THE CAPTAIN'S SECRET BABY

A.J. WYNTER

ALSO BY A.J. WYNTER

ONE
BRONWYN

THE ENGINE SPUTTERED and I felt the boat surge forward before it lost power. "No. No. No." I pulled back on the throttle and the boat settled in the still water in the middle of the bay, smoke billowing into the blue sky. "Shit," I whispered under my breath.

Even though the engine had already quit running, I turned off the key. The waves from the wake caught up to us and rocked the boat as I made my way to the stern. Smoke seeped from the engine compartment as I fumbled with the antique hinges to open it.

"What are you doing?" My friend, Tess, stretched her tanned arms over her head and looked at me over her oversized Jackie O glasses.

"Ouch!" The hinge released and, in the process, bent my nail backward. It felt like every drop of blood in my body had rushed to my thumb. "Ow. Ow. Ow." I shook my hand and leaned over the side of the boat to plunge my hand into the cold water of Lake Casper. I coughed as the wind shifted direction and the smoke from the engine wrapped around my entire body before blowing further across the lake. I wrapped the bottom of my silk dress around my thumb and managed to open the other clasp. I tried to lift the lid. It wouldn't budge. It turns out that mahogany is very heavy. "Can you help me?" It was awkward trying to lift the lid to the engine compartment with one functioning hand and the other wrapped in red silk.

Tess examined her nails. "Let's just call someone." She reached into her Yves St. Laurent bag and pulled out her cell phone.

"What if the engine is on fire?" I pointed to the black smoke.

Tess's eyebrows rose high above her glasses. "Fire?"

"Fire makes smoke. Help me."

Tess rushed to the back of the classic wooden boat and together we were able to raise the cover. The smoke curled out from deep within the jumble of pipes and wires, but thankfully I didn't see any flames. Tess turned and coughed into her arm. She lifted her glasses and wiped at her watery eyes with her pink manicured fingers.

I pointed to her phone. "It doesn't look like we have to abandon ship. Now, we can call for help."

Tess coughed. "Who should I call?"

I stepped to the front of the boat and took a deep breath of fresh air. "Let me think."

"What about your house manager?"

I turned to face what was supposed to be one of my best friends. "Do you remember earlier today? The part where I told you I wasn't supposed to take this boat to the club?"

"Riiiiiight." Tess nodded. "But we looked super cute pulling up in it."

We had looked cute. Heads had definitely turned – two supermodels getting out of a classic wooden boat at the private Lake Casper Club.

The boat was a well-known fixture on the Lake Casper

antique circuit and my parents had been offered half a million dollars to sell it the year before. They never would, *Calliope* had been in the Yates family since the turn of the twentieth century, purchased the same year that my great-great-grandparents had built our cottage, The Yates Estate.

I sucked my throbbing thumb as I racked my brain, trying to figure out what to do about the boat and wondering about karma. Is this what happened when I disobeyed my parents? They specifically told me not to take *Calliope* from her berth in the boathouse. Why had I let Tess convince me it was a good idea? I knew that I could return the boat without a scratch, and they'd never know the difference, but it had never crossed my mind that there might be something wrong with her. If I called the house manager, she would tell my parents and I was already in their bad books. I flopped into the captain's seat. "Why don't we call Brandon?" I suggested.

"Davenport?" Tess asked, but was already scrolling through her phone. "He was heading to the first tee when we left."

"If he wants to sleep with you, he'll waltz right off that golf course, get in his boat, and rescue us."

Tess had rejected Brandon's advances all summer and it had driven him crazy. She'd had her eyes on one of the New York Thunder pro hockey players.

Tess nodded with a slight smirk on her face and jabbed at her phone. A puzzled look came over her face as she tried again and then held her phone up into the sky. "Zero bars of service." She walked from one side of the boat to the other, her eyes trained on the screen.

The engine smoke had thinned, and the only sound was the lapping of the water against the hull. "What are we going to do?" Panic had quickly crept into Tess's voice.

"Let me think." The slight rocking of the boat and the noxious fumes were a recipe for disaster in my stomach.

"Bronwyn." Tess's voice rose an octave higher than usual. "We're stuck out here." She shielded her eyes with her hand. "It's so hot. We'll get dehydrated."

I inhaled and tried to keep my salmon and mixed greens lunch from making an unwelcome appearance. "Tess. It's Lake Casper. Not the ocean. Someone will come by and give us a tow to the marina, or..." I didn't want to think of the alternative and the damage it would cause to *Calliope*, "We'll drift to shore. If you're worried about dying in the next two hours, feel free to drink the lake water."

Tess shriveled her nose and fanned her face.

She was right though; the heat was intense. August in Laketown was either hot and humid or cool and rainy. So far this year, it had been more like the Serengeti and a rush of nausea ripped through my body like a tidal wave. "Oh no." I clamped my hand over my mouth and threw my upper body over the starboard side of the boat, barfing my fifty-dollar salad into the lake.

"Don't." Tess turned away from me. "You're going to make me puke too."

I waited for my stomach to calm down and then scooped some water into my mouth to rinse it out.

"I can't believe you get seasick." Tess's voice was muffled as she still had her hand clamped firmly on her mouth. "Don't you spend months on a yacht?"

With shaky hands, I eased into the captain's chair. I wasn't seasick. I had sailed the Mediterranean every year since I was a little kid, but I wasn't ready to tell Tess, or anyone, the truth – just yet. "I think it was the smell from the smoke and the heat."

Tess nodded.

I pointed to the rear bench seat of the boat. "There might be a hat or a blanket or something under the cushion."

Tess retrieved a striped cotton blanket and the two of us

held it over our heads. As twenty-something, aka ancient models, neither of us could afford to have skin damage. "My arms are getting tired." Tess dropped her end of the blanket tent into her lap.

"It's been thirty seconds." I shook my head. "Here. Give me your end." I gestured with my hand, and she handed me the fringed edge of the blanket. I leaned over the windshield and tucked the side under the windshield wipers and draped the other edge over the backrests of the front seats. We huddled on the floor under the blanket, both of us with our phones in hand, eyes glued to the screen waiting for the arrival of a bar on the screen.

A boat droned by in the distance, and I crawled from the tent to wave my arms in the air, but they didn't alter course. Five minutes later, the wake from their boat reached ours, and Tess and I rocked miserably in our tent.

"A round of golf at the club takes about four hours," Tess mused. "Brandon and Tad have to come this way to get to their cottages."

I glanced at my Rolex. "That means we've got three and a half hours to go."

"And that's if they don't stop at the club for a beer after their round."

I couldn't sit upright any longer and laid on the floor of the boat. "Ugggghhh," I groaned. "I can't believe nobody has stopped."

Tess peeked out from under the blanket. "I can't see any boats, anywhere."

She leaned on her elbows and sighed. "I could go for some prosecco right about now."

"Me too." It wasn't a lie. I sure could have used a cold bubbly glass of something. It had been three and a half months since a drop of alcohol had passed my lips, but not one of my friends noticed that I had offered to be the designated driver every time we went out. It was the perfect excuse not to drink and the one that I had used that day. Unfortunately, I chose to drive the half a million-dollar hunk of junk that was now drifting down the middle of Lake Casper.

Tess checked her phone. "Nothing." She dropped it onto her flat stomach. Luckily voluminous dresses were my style and so far, my belly didn't look any different from the outside – although it sure felt different on the inside. "When we get in range should I call Tyler?" Tess asked. Tyler was the pro hockey player Tess had been lusting after all summer.

"Aren't you leaving in a couple of weeks?"

"Yeah." Tess picked at an invisible piece of lint on her linen shirt. "But you can do a lot in two weeks." She grinned conspiratorially. "What's the latest with McManus?"

I shrugged. Six months ago, I would've given my right arm for a date with Jake McManus. He was exactly what I liked – older, sophisticated, rich, and hot. He was the perfect man for me, and I had spent the past two summers pining for him. Ever since my ex-fiancé left me, I'd been searching for the perfect man to have at my side. One that I could bring home to my parents – and more importantly, my grand-parents.

"I told Jake that I would be free for dinner sometime this week."

"Bronwyn." Tess's voice was harsh. "Why do you keep putting him off? The guy has been trying to buy you dinner all summer."

I shot her one of my best fake smiles. Luckily, I was an expert at them and she was really bad at reading people. "That's why he keeps calling. I keep saying no."

Tess laid down on the floor next to me. "You're so good at that. If Tyler asked me out, I'd probably end up sleeping with him in the car on the way to the restaurant. I need to adopt some of your self-control."

If she only knew that there was a baby in my belly. One that was put there from a one-night stand. Well, technically it was a series of one-night stands over the past two years, so she might have something different to say about my level of control.

"I forgot that you've got your little townie friend with benefits." Tess laughed.

My cheeks burned, and I hoped that under the shelter of the red and white stripes, it wasn't obvious.

"What was his name again? Is he still around?"

I couldn't bring myself to say his name. "I don't know. I haven't seen him this summer."

It was the truth. I hadn't seen him since the spring. May to be exact.

"You're something else, Bronwyn. You could have any guy on this lake, and you chose to get down and dirty with a Laketownie."

I smacked her thigh lazily. "You and the girls are the only people who know about that." I sat up. "You haven't told anyone, have you?"

Tess's body rocked into mine as some rolling waves met the side of the boat. "Of course not. That's not something anyone would want to get out."

I exhaled. "Thanks. You know what the rumor mill is like here – and it's worse for—"

"Us?" she laughed. "I'm surprised the paparazzi haven't zoomed up beside us to take photos of the heir to the Yates Petroleum fortune, stranded in the middle of a lake.

"Nah, they're cowering on the shore somewhere with their super lenses. Not helping."

Tess laughed. "They'd let us die out here and document the whole thing, wouldn't they?"

"Yep." A sad laugh escaped because it was true.

"What makes you think that little Laketownie isn't bragging all over town that he's banged Bronwyn Yates?"

I hated that she kept calling him little but defending him would certainly throw up some red flags. "He's not like that."

"Sure. Until one of the paparazzi offers him money for the story."

"Mmmm." My reply was non-committal. I had been sleeping with one of the Laketown Otters on and off for the past two years and I knew him better than I'd known my ex-fiancé. My Laketownie was hot as hell, made me cry with laughter one minute, and scream in ecstasy the next. He wasn't the full package though: he was an uneducated, small-town jock who sometimes used the word *ain't*. But if there were a bedroom package, he had it all. He was the perfect mixture of rough and wild and sweet and giving.

The rocking of the boat must have lulled my exhausted pregnant body to sleep because I awoke to Tess shaking my arm.

"Bronwyn, there's a boat coming." She hopped to her feet and grabbed the blanket to wave it in the air. "They're coming over here." She was practically squealing and stamping her feet with excitement.

I draped my arm over my eyes to protect them from the sudden assault of the sun's rays. Without looking, I could hear the deep throaty sound of another wooden boat approaching. "It's a nice boat." Tess relayed the information to me as I peeled myself from the floor. I adjusted my Ray-Bans and joined Tess in waving to the guy as he approached. Everyone knew *Calliope* and I shielded my eyes as I tried to identify the boat as it approached. It looked like the Hawthorne's cruiser. Mr. Hawthorne was a tech billionaire and a friend of my father's.

"Shit." I shook my head, but I wasn't going to complain. I

could already feel the tightness in my face from being out in the elements for too long. Mr. Hawthorne was sure to tell my father that he'd had to rescue *Calliope*, but I would rather face the wrath of my father than spend the night floating on Lake Casper.

As he approached my breath caught in my throat. It wasn't Mr. Hawthorne. It was way worse. Ten million times worse.

"I think it's a mechanic," Tess whispered.

It definitely was a mechanic. He was wearing the green mechanic shirt from the Lake Casper Marina and had a huge grin on his face.

Tess whispered, even though there was no way he could've heard us over the engine noise. "Isn't that your little townie?"

I didn't have to read the name embroidered on his uniform to know that the man rescuing us was none other than Dylan Moss. The man whose baby I was hiding beneath my silk dress.

TWO
DYLAN

THE WAKE behind Mr. Hawthorne's boat was small and flat as I pushed the throttle down. I loved how the guttural growl of the engine and the wind whipping in my ears made me forget, temporarily, that I was working. The only reminder was the sweat on my back underneath the heavy-duty mechanic's shirt. I'd rolled up the sleeves as far as I could and put my Otters' hat on backward to stop my hair from whipping me in the face as I made sure the modifications to the boat's engine were working properly.

A recognizable silhouette on the horizon caught my attention. *Calliope*, one of the most iconic Lake Casper boats was unmoving in the middle of Anchor Bay, a big and uninhabited section of the lake. I squinted my eyes behind my sunglasses and tried to see if the driver was visible. Seeing *Calliope* in the wild, and not in a boat show was a rare treat. The Yates had a fleet of boats and from what I'd heard *Calliope* sat protected in their massive boathouse for most of the summer.

Wishing that I had a pair of binoculars in the boat, I altered course, steering into Anchor Bay and slowing as I approached. A striped blanket was draped over the windshield and there was no sign of life in the boat. It bobbed and rocked as I neared and a pretty girl that looked familiar emerged from underneath the blanket. She flailed her arms in the universal "we need help!" wave and I gave her a nod, wondering where I had seen her before.

I pulled up alongside *Calliope* and tossed a couple of bumpers over the side to protect both crafts. As I tossed a buoyant line to the girl, a second appeared. One that I certainly knew. One that I had seen naked on more than one occasion.

I took a deep breath. It was too late to turn back, so I put on a huge fake smile and pretended that I was happy to see the snobby woman who had ghosted me in the spring.

"You ladies need a hand?"

I caught Bronwyn's eyes taking in my backward hat and mechanic's uniform. She knew what I did for a living, but it was the first time she'd ever seen me in my natural habitat. My natural, greasy, blue-collar habitat. I took the hat off and pretended to bow to the two of them like a butler might in an old-timey movie. I made sure to put the hat on, brim forward, when I put it over my flat wind-whipped mop that hadn't been cut all summer.

"The boat won't go." The friend, whose name I couldn't recall, but remembered meeting at Valerock after a few too many pilsner's years ago said.

I tried not to laugh and pressed my lips together at the all too familiar, very undiagnostic description of the issue. Bronwyn's eyes met mine, the blue of her eyes was the same color as the lake behind her, and equally as cold, snuffing out the laugh. She crossed her arms and her red dress whipped in the wind around her - she looked both gorgeous and terrifying at the same time. "Smoke came out of the engine and then it stopped." Her voice was cold, definitely not the same husky voice who had whispered for me to fuck her harder the last time I'd seen her.

I shivered even though the breeze swirling around us was over eighty degrees. "How long ago?" It was time to get down to business. There were clearly not going to be any pleasantries.

The women exchanged a glance and the one I didn't know shrugged.

"About an hour or so."

I tugged on the line that had landed on the passenger seat of the *Calliope*. "Can one of you hold onto the end of the rope?"

Bronwyn nodded and I could feel the tension in the line as she grasped it with both hands. This connection was the only one we'd had in months and I'm not the gushy romantic type at all. Hell, Bronwyn and I had only been friends with benefits, but feeling her on the other end of the rope, felt good. I blinked hard behind my sunglasses and wondered what the hell was happening to me. She'd had her fun and obviously, it was over. I wondered if I would've gotten tired of showing up every time she texted, like a lovesick puppy dog. Fuck that, I wasn't a lovesick puppy dog. It was what it was, and I was a horn dog, getting what I wanted. Not the other way around.

"Got it?" I asked.

Bronwyn nodded and I gently pulled the rope, inching the boats closer together. "That's good," I instructed as the bumpers did their job. I held onto the side of *Calliope*. "Permission to come aboard?"

A smile appeared on Bronwyn's face, and her eyes lit up, if for only a brief second.

But her friend rolled her eyes. "Can you just get in here and fix it." She fanned her pink chest, and I was secretly glad that the snobby bitch was going to have a gnarly sunburn. I spent most of my days working in the back of the marina and didn't have to deal with the wealthy boat owners, and moments like this made me very glad that was the case.

"Let me help you." Bronwyn accompanied me to the rear of the boat and to my surprise grabbed one side of the engine compartment with her perfectly manicured nails. Together we opened it and instantly I was overwhelmed with the smell of burnt oil. I leaned into the cavernous engine hold and inspected a few of the hoses and wires. I pulled the rag out of my back pocket and checked the oil level - it was just as I thought. I wiped my hands as clean as I could with the rag. "I'm going to have to tow you to the marina." Bronwyn nodded and buckled the clasp on the compartment.

"Tess," Bronwyn shouted.

Tess. Her name had been on the tip of my tongue. It was so close to my sister's name, Jess, I wouldn't forget it now. She was sitting with the blanket wrapped over her shoulders. The Hawthorne's boat was drifting down the bay behind her.

"What?" she looked up from examining her nails.

Bronwyn pointed to the boat. "You were supposed to hold on!"

Tess craned her head and when she looked at us her eyes were wide, but I couldn't tell if it was with embarrassment or fear.

"For fuck's sake," I growled.

"What?" Tess repeated. "No one told me to hold on."

I shook my head and tried not to swear ` and that small act took every ounce of self-restraint I had in my body. She was playing fully into the entitled rich girl stereotype.

"Tess." There was exasperation in Bronwyn's voice. She shielded her eyes with her hand, and I thought that I saw a shimmer of a tear in the corner of her eye.

I whispered "fuck" under my breath one more time and kicked off my steel-toed Blundstone's, unsnapped my mechanic's shirt, and peeled off my sweaty white t-shirt before launching myself into Lake Casper. Years of winning the swimming regatta had paid off and my efficient front crawl had me at the helm of the boat in under a minute. I hoisted myself onto the boat, swearing as pools of water formed at my feet from my soaking wet jeans. The boss wasn't going to be happy. I held my breath as I turned the key, exhaling with gratitude when she started with a roar. The last thing we needed was two broken-down boats in the center of the cell phone dead zone of Anchor Bay. The seat squelched as I sat on the expensive upholstery. I looked at the drifting boat with the two women and had to make a choice. Piss off my boss by ruining the seats of this boat or rescue the damsels in distress in my skivvies.

"Fuck it." That seemed to be my motto for the day.

I stood and peeled the wet jeans off my body and squeezed out as much water as I could before putting the boat in gear to navigate to the broken-down boat. Even though it was hot, goosebumps spread down my arms as the wind started to blow. I looked behind me and saw dark clouds on the horizon. "Shit."

This underwear rescue had to happen. And fast.

THREE

BRONWYN

WITH THE LINES TIED, Dylan towed *Calliope* south down the lake. The trip to the marina took twenty-five minutes but felt more like three days.

"I think I can swim faster than this," Tess whined as she twirled her hair.

Dylan ignored Tess's complaint. She had the striped blanket wrapped around her body. But unlike earlier when she was protecting herself from the sun, the weather had turned, and she was keeping herself warm. I glanced at the horizon and shivered, then focused my eyes on my grand-parents' pride and joy as she was towed along behind us. When we exited Anchor Bay and had cell reception, Dylan called the marina and barked orders for the staff to get ready for our arrival.

"Can't we go any faster?" Tess pouted.

"Have you got somewhere to be?" The Dylan I thought I knew, the one that was always in a good mood was nowhere to be found. This version had been surly the entire ride.

"Actually, I do." Tess crossed her arm, hugging the blanket tighter around her body.

A sudden change in the wind direction caused the skirt of my dress to billow up around me. Dylan turned in his seat, his eyes unfriendly. Like a bull. I wanted to explain why I hadn't returned any of his calls, and why I hadn't responded to his text messages, especially the super sweet ones. I tucked the skirt under my legs, both for warmth and to avoid flashing my La Perla underwear that was pinching into my waist. It was the first thing that had felt tight on my body as my stomach started to get a little less flat.

My eyes met his and he saw me rubbing the goosebumps on my arms and nonchalantly nudged the throttle down. *Calliope* cut through the wake with ease, and he sped up a little more. I wondered if he was worried about getting caught in the storm because of us, or because of the boats.

"Are you cold?" he shouted over the engine noise.

I shook my head. "I'm fine," but my lips quivered as I spoke.

He narrowed his lips and hung his head as if he was frustrated with me. It had been a total lie, I wasn't cold... I was freezing.

"Here." He unbuttoned his shirt and handed it to me.

Tess raised her eyebrows as I slipped into the faded canvas shirt with the grease stains on the front, but I was so cold I would've put on a blanket from a dog kennel.

Despite its appearance, the shirt didn't stink. It was the opposite. I curled into a ball as I kept an eye on *Calliope*, tucking my knees under the fabric that smelled like Dylan's shampoo, campfire smoke, and a little bit of oil. Exactly the way my pillows smelled after he left in the morning. I pretended like I was resting my eyes on my knees, only to tuck my face into the collar and inhale Dylan's scent as deeply as I could. What is it about a scent that can transport you to another time and place? With my head tucked into Dylan's shirt, I was transported to the last time I was in his arms, marveling as I dragged my fingertip along his sinewy forearm, toned from years of slapshot after slapshot. We had been comparing our embarrassing music tastes, the artists that we secretly adored but would never admit to loving. I could almost feel his chest under my cheek, laughing when I disclosed that I loved listening to early Justin Bieber. When he disclosed that he had a soft spot for Celine Dion I turned over, sure that I'd see that sly smirk on his face, the one he made when he was joking, but it wasn't there. I'd crawled up his body. "Ooh, la, la, Dylan," I whispered in my best French accent, honed from years of walking the runways of Paris.

"Hellooooo, Celine," he'd growled and tossed me onto my back.

The static from the marina crew's radio interrupted the scene playing in my mind.

"Miss." One of the teenaged boys held out his hand to help me from the boat. I untucked my knees from Dylan's shirt, grateful for the warm hand pulling me to the dock. Another of the employees opened an umbrella just as the first drops fell heavily from the sky. "Come with me." His voice cracked and his face flushed with embarrassment.

"Thank you." I hooked my hand above his elbow. He jumped at my touch and turned the same shade of red as my dress.

He recovered and crooked his arm like a gentleman. "Right this way, Miss Yates."

It wasn't until we reached the end of the dock that I realized my shoes and handbag were still tucked under *Calliope*'s bow. "My shoes." I turned to see that there were at least ten employees of the marina working together to winch *Calliope* onto a trailer. I couldn't help but laugh, my family's boat was more of a celebrity than I was.

My young gentleman made a call on his radio and as the voice on the other end confirmed that my Manolos would be delivered promptly. Tess was being escorted to the marina by another golf shirt-clad employee, but she'd been wise enough to grab her accessories when we'd abandoned ship. I had been too flustered by Dylan's presence.

"Eeeeee." Tess squealed as the rain intensified, bouncing off the wooden dock as it turned into a downpour. The poor guy holding my umbrella was instantly soaked.

"You can get underneath if you'd like." I shifted to make room under the golf umbrella for him.

He shook his head. "I'm fine. Your shoes should be here shortly." Raindrops were dripping from his eyelashes.

"Come on." I winced as I took a step onto the sharp gravel.

"Miss Yates," he protested, but I had already stepped from the shelter of the umbrella, and he had to take two giant steps to catch up. The stones hurt my feet, but I wasn't that much of a princess that I needed a young kid to stand in the pouring rain while I waited for my designer sandals, which likely would've been more dangerous, possibly entering ankle-breaking territory – on the gravel.

With my dress gripped in my left hand, I focused on the ground as we made our way to the shelter of the marina. I didn't hear the footsteps running towards us. I saw Dylan, his white T-shirt and jeans, soaking wet, with my strappy sandals looped over his thick fingers, my handbag across his chest.

"Jesus, Sam. You're letting her walk on this stuff?" His voice was low and angry.

"She said—" Sam protested.

Dylan thrust the shoes at the boy. "Here. Take her damn shoes."

Sam released my arm so he could grab the shoes and before I knew what had happened, Dylan Moss scooped me up in his arms, honeymoon style. I instinctively gripped onto his neck and curled tightly against him as he ran, no, sprinted, his boots crunching on the gravel beneath us while his breath rasped loudly, but efficiently by my ear.

Nestling into his neck would've been easy. Inhaling the source of the smell from the collar of his shirt was within smelling distance. But I didn't. Getting close to Dylan would be a colossal mistake, and now I had to think of someone besides myself. The last time we'd been together I'd teased him about his scraggly playoff beard, which I secretly liked. Today his sharp jawbone was clean-shaven and more chiseled than any of the models in my last runway show.

When we reached the shelter of the marina, Dylan set me down and walked away without saying anything.

Tess sidled up beside me. "That was kind of hot," she whispered. "Are you sure you don't want to ride that guy one more time?" I glanced around the room to see if anyone had heard and was mortified to see that Sam's cheeks were so red now, they were almost purple.

"Tess," I hissed and elbowed her. She looked at Sam and shrugged.

Sam handed me my shoes. "Miss…" his voice croaked.

"Thank you, Sam." I automatically reached for my handbag to give him a tip, but it wasn't there. I looked past the boats into the back office and could see the leather strap slung over Dylan's broad back.

Sam held up his hands. He knew I was searching for tip money. "Let me know if you need anything else," he said, then walked away at a brisk pace.

I'm pretty sure he would've put the shoes on my feet for me if I'd asked. I slipped the sandals on my feet and did up the tiny buckles, noticing that I had to move to the next bigger hole in the leather strap. Great, the first sign of this pregnancy was uncomfortable lace panties, the second, sore feet. I shook my head and stood. Now I towered over every man in the garage - except the one that was wearing my purse.

"How are we going to get home?" Tess asked. "There's no Uber here."

Tess was technically a year older than me and had attended college – so she should've been more worldly, but she seemed like a child at times. College was still on my to-do list – after my modeling career was over.

"I'll call someone." I didn't roll my eyes, even though I wanted to. My heels clicked on the concrete as I wove between the room full of boats, my eyes trained on Dylan's back until something shiny caught my eye. Outside the door to the office where my purse snatcher was having what looked to be a very intense discussion, stood a wooden boat, but this one had a shape as I'd never seen before. Its gunwales arched up at the bow and the stern, it was unusual and didn't fit in with the Lake Casper boat scene.

I dragged my finger along the wood, sanded so smooth it felt silkier than my dress, which was actual silk. The cuff of Dylan's shirt fell over my fingertips, startling me. I had forgotten was wearing it. Even though it was providing me with warmth, I pulled at it, hearing the satisfying pop of the snaps as I ripped it off and strode into the office. "Your shirt." I held it out in front of me. I didn't care that I was inter-rupting the conversation.

Dylan and a man with a white mustache stared at me. Mr. White Mustache took off his hat and reached out his hand. "Miss Yates, a pleasure to meet you. I'm Floyd Winkman."

"Nice to meet you." His hand looked permanently stained from oil but was surprisingly soft as I shook it. "I presume you've met Dylan Moss." His caterpillar-like eyebrows raised as he looked between us.

"I have had the pleasure." I thrust the shirt at Dylan again. "You have my purse."

Dylan took the shirt and put his hand to his chest. "I didn't realize..."

Floyd hacked out a laugh. "I thought it was your new look."

Dylan cast a glare at the man, shrugged the purse over his head, and tossed it at me. I wasn't ready and it bounced off my fingertips and fell to the floor.

"Dylan." Floyd sounded exasperated.

"Catch much?" Dylan gave me the smile that used to make my heart flutter.

"It's alright, Mr. Winkman." I scooped the bag up from the floor, brushed it off, and glared at Dylan.

"Floyd?" A woman with hair just as white as Floyd's peeked into the office. "There's a call I think you should take."

Floyd nodded. "Thanks, Thelma. Miss Yates, I have to take this call. You wait right here." He patted one of the leather chairs. "I'll have someone from the marina give you and your friend a ride home. *Calliope* isn't going anywhere anytime soon."

My heart sank, but I nodded. My feet were throbbing as I eased myself into the chair.

"Are you okay?" Dylan asked.

I smoothed the skirt over my legs and tried not to shiver. "I'm fine."

"You look like an eighty-year-old woman with hemorrhoids."

"Fuck off, Dylan." It was my turn to throw my purse. But damn him and his lightning-fast reflexes. He caught it before it hit his face.

He tilted his head and handed the purse back. "Seriously, Bron. Are you alright?" He took a seat in the chair next to me. I shifted away from him, knowing what close proximity to his scent did to my body.

"I said. I'm fine." I crossed my arms across my chest.

Dylan reclined in the chair, kicked one foot in front of him, and laced his fingers behind his head. "You might be fine. But you certainly did a number on *Calliope*."

My breath caught in my throat. "Is it bad? I thought she just broke down."

"It's hard to say yet. Floyd's the expert on those engines, but from what I saw, she might require a complete rebuild."

"A. Complete…." My voice faded.

"Rebuild." Dylan finished.

"Shit," I muttered.

He furrowed his brow. "What does it matter to you?"

I couldn't get into the details with Dylan. The only heir to the Yates fortune was an unmarried, uneducated, embarrassment to the Yates name. Now that embarrassment had just killed *Calliope*. How could I explain that to him? He'd never understand.

I leaned over the arm of the chair to swing the office door closed. "Dylan. I need you to help me."

He didn't look at me, but I could see his eyebrows rise. He maintained his leisure-like posture and I wondered if he was enjoying my neediness. "Help you? Like more help than rescuing you and your friend from dehydration and heatstroke?"

I needed to speak his language. "Have you ever been in trouble with your parents?"

His hands dropped from behind his head, and I realized the terrible mistake I had made. "I'm sorry, I forgot."

His head hung, but only momentarily. "You forgot that my parents are dead."

I rested my hand on his, but when I went to squeeze it, he pulled away. "I'm sorry," I whispered.

The door swung open, and Floyd stepped into the office. "Miss Yates." He had a clipboard with him and flipped a few pages. "Your house manager. Is that who I should call with details about the boat repair?"

"No." I practically shot out of the chair. "She's off for a little bit." I lied. "Can you call me? I'll relay the information to my parents."

Floyd scribbled a note on the paper and took down my phone number. "I'll have more details tomorrow."

He looked past me. "The water taxi is all fueled up. Can you take Miss Yates and her friend home?"

I couldn't see Dylan, but I could hear the growl in his voice. "Isn't that Sam's job?"

"We've got a fuel shipment coming in that he's helping with that. Keys are in the boat." Floyd's no-nonsense approach was refreshing, but I wasn't looking forward to yet another boat ride with Dylan.

Floyd sat at his desk. "I said the keys are in the boat." He didn't look up from his paperwork.

"Your chariot awaits." Dylan gave his boss a side glance and opened the door for me, gesturing like a clown.

"Smarten up, Dylan," Floyd rasped. I tried to keep the smile from spreading across my face as I walked away, but sometimes it had a mind of its own.

"What are you grinning at?" Tess asked. She was sitting on the end of a dock, her feet crossed over the side of a wakeboard boat.

"Nothing. We've got a ride home."

Tess stood. "I was hoping that the owner of this boat would give us a ride home." She pointed at the name on the back of the boat. It wasn't a name, just a number. And, you didn't have to be a hockey fan to know that number 74 was Jake McManus' retired number.

Tess was either a really good friend or a really bad one. Was she hoping that Jake McManus would show up for her or me?

I felt a surge of nausea and realized it didn't matter. "Our ride is over there." I pointed to the water taxi dock where Dylan had already started up one of the boats.

"Pity," Tess pouted.

Dylan helped both Tess and me into the water taxi and handed us two Lake Casper windbreaker jackets to wear. Dylan knew how to get to my cottage. He'd shown up several nights over the last couple of years by water but had to get directions from Tess to hers.

Tess protested about being dropped off first. "I was hoping to see the decorating changes you've done to your bunkie." Tess waited for Dylan to help her out of the boat onto her dock then she gave me a sly smile. "I guess the mechanic will be the first one to see your new place."

I wondered if it was the pregnancy hormones, or if Tess had always been a terrible person.

"The renovations aren't done yet," I muttered. "You'll be the first to see the bunkie when it's done." I shot her a weary smile, and she blew me back a kiss. I had effectively killed two birds with one stone. I'd placated Tess and ensured Dylan wouldn't expect an invite upstairs.

FOUR
DYLAN

BRONWYN HAD GROWN up around boats and it showed. Even though we had taken the crappy water taxi, she took off her ridiculous high-heeled sandals for the ride. After we got rid of her friend, who I was convinced was either dumb or evil, I wanted to ask her the question that had been on my mind for the past few months – but I was waiting for the right time.

She held onto her hair as I ran the water taxi at top speed down the middle of Lake Casper. The Yates family compound loomed large at the north end of the lake. It was built in the era when cottages blended into their surroundings, and in old photos, it had been painted the same color green as the trees. Today, it was a light yellow and its bronze cupolas could be seen for miles.

As I reversed the engine to sidle perfectly at the end of her dock, she leaped out of the boat like a cat.

"Bron…" I had been trying so hard not to call her by her nickname. Shit. "Wyn," I added quickly.

"Did all the pucks to the head give you a stutter?" she asked.

I didn't blame her. I had been an immature jerk, and she was giving it back to me.

"Ha. Ha." I drew out the words and waited for her to walk away. She took off her sunglasses and slowly folded their arms. It seemed like she was lingering, waiting for something. "What? Do you need to be carried to your fancy bunkhouse?"

She bit her lip and her dress flared as she spun and walked away. I rolled my eyes. The woman couldn't walk down a dock without putting on her ridiculous model strut. She threw her arm in the air and yelled. "Byeeeee Dylan."

"Wait," I shouted. The dress flared again, but this time a breeze caught it from below and the entire skirt blew up in front of her face, giving me the perfect view of her lacy panties. She battled with her dress and managed to hold it in her fists at her thighs.

I shifted in the seat, the millisecond view of her panties, pink ones that didn't match her dress had gotten me hard.

"What?" Her voice had an edge to it.

Why didn't you call? Did you not get the text messages I sent? What about that voicemail where I told you I couldn't wait to see you? "Your purse."

I snatched it from the seat beside me and tossed it to her. This time she caught it.

What was I thinking? She had already proven herself to be incapable of catching anything, and if she didn't already hate me, which I think she did, tossing her purse into the lake would've ensured me a spot on her shit list.

"Unbelievable." She put her purse strap over her shoulder. "I don't know what your problem is Dylan, but…" her voice faded.

"But what?" Our wake had caught up to us and I gripped the dock boards with my fingers as the boat rolled, bumping into the dock.

My eyes were glued to hers and hers to mine. I questioned whose were angrier looking, hoping that the answer was mine.

She gave me a dismissive wave. "Just go."

She was much meaner. I wasn't ready to go. "I was leaving. You don't get to tell me when to come or go."

"Go then."

"I'm leaving."

She didn't move and neither did I.

What was she doing? My cock was hard and pressing against my damp jeans. Her steely gaze did the opposite of what it should do. It made me want her. Without thinking, I launched myself from the boat and my work boots thudded on the wooden pier. I wrapped my arms around her waist and pulled her against me. I felt her sharp exhale on my neck from the force of our chests colliding. And then I kissed her.

And she kissed me back.

FIVE
BRONWYN

THE WIND WHIPPED, causing my skirt to threaten another Marilyn Monroe moment. "You need to leave." I pushed Dylan away with my hands, even though I wanted to press every inch of my body against every inch of his.

Dylan's eyes were pools of stormy blue when I stepped away from him.

"Why have you been avoiding me?" His voice rumbled like distant thunder.

I opened my mouth to respond but didn't have an answer. I didn't want to lie to him, but I didn't want to tell him the truth either. "It's a mistake. We can't keep doing this."

He stepped toward me, but I took a step back and the fight disappeared from his eyes. "Whatever," he muttered and turned away.

My mind screamed, *Dylan, don't go*, but my body did nothing. "I'm sorry," I whispered.

He jumped into the boat. "Yeah. Me too."

The outboard engine started in a puff of smoke and Dylan hammered down the throttle, leaving me behind in a cloud of engine smoke and waves banging against the pier.

I managed to keep the tears at bay until the water taxi disappeared behind Danger Island. I touched my fingertips to my lips which still felt like they were buzzing with electricity. For something so bad, kissing him felt so damn good.

I used to think people were full of it when they said someone's touch made them melt, but that day, when Dylan's hands grabbed my hips, I could've dripped through the slats in the dock and all that would've been left was a pool of my red silk dress on the wooden planks.

The sound of a car approaching made my breath catch in my throat. I was supposed to be alone this weekend. If my parents had seen Dylan Moss kissing me, my inheritance was as good as gone. And it was all that I had.

I swiped angrily at the tears on my face, but more just took their place. Damn hormones. I thought to myself and made my way to my bunkie. As I passed the main cottage, I remembered that my parents had taken the helicopter when they left.

As if their spidey senses warned them that their daughter was kissing a townie, the sound of a helicopter echoed across the water. I groaned and picked up the pace, bypassing the main cottage.

The screen door slammed behind me as I made it to the refuge of my bunkie. I flopped onto the couch and tried to forget the feel of Dylan's lips on mine.

What was I going to do?

Spending all this time at the family cottage was supposed to give me clarity, but it only made me more confused. If this were the 1960s, my parents would've shipped me off somewhere far, far away to give birth. But it wasn't the sixties and even though they were upset with me for getting pregnant, they were happy that the Yates family line would continue.

The hunger pangs couldn't be ignored any longer. I had thrown up the only thing I had eaten that day and while I was used to going hungry, I wasn't going to subject my baby to that feeling. I rested my hand on my belly and pulled myself to a seated position. Dylan was right, I was moving like an old lady.

I padded to the fridge to see if my housekeeper had left any meals for me. Everyone in the family had a personal housekeeper, and my friends joked that I had my nanny. My housekeeper, Lisa was a kid from Laketown High. My parents had wanted to hire someone more experienced, but I liked the fact that she was young and needed the opportunity.

The big tip I left her every week ensured that my fridge was fully stocked, and it was always in the back of my mind that Lisa could easily spread my news all through the town, but I trusted her. I shuffled the glass containers around on the shelves, praying for something cheesy and crunchy to appear, fully knowing that cheesy and crunchy were not on the list of approved meals.

"Dammit." I slammed the fridge door so hard the condiments rattled inside. My stomach growled again, and it wasn't a want, it was a need - my first pregnancy craving. It wasn't one of those weird pregnancy cravings. No, I just wanted a pizza, a pizza with pepperoni and cheese and a thick crust and lots of sauce. Nothing fancy, no thin crust, no gluten-free, I wanted the real deal, and I wanted it yesterday.

I texted Lisa and asked her advice on where to order a pizza. While I waited for her response, I slipped out of my lace panties and rubbed at the mark on my hips where the thin waistband had been cutting into my sides.

My phone buzzed and I smiled. Another pro for hiring a young person - she texted back almost instantly. The news wasn't good though, there was only one pizza parlor in town and, they didn't deliver on Tuesday.

If I wanted pizza, I was either going to have to make it or go into Laketown.

My phone chimed with another text. Lisa was offering to bring the pizza to me. As much as I wanted to bite into cheese and bread, I couldn't ask her to rush out on her day off.

I wasn't my parents.

I replied to Lisa and told her not to put on her delivery hat, then slipped into a pair of ballet flats, grabbed my purse, and headed to the carriage house. I felt like a kid sneaking out to see her boyfriend in the middle of the night.

"Bron. Honey."

I froze and turned. "

Hi, Mom."

She was standing in the doorway with her arms crossed. If she could've moved her face, her brows would've furrowed. My mom had enough stuff injected into her to ensure that no emotion would ever show on her face again.

"Are you going somewhere?" she asked.

"I'm heading into town." I didn't want to lie to my mom.

Her gaze traveled up and down my body. "I thought that we talked about this."

I sighed. "I can't hide here forever."

"Hide. Here?" she spread her arms wide. "You have everything you need here."

Not pizza.

I smoothed my hands down the front of my dress. "I'm not showing yet. I thought it was okay to be seen until, you know…" I couldn't bring myself to say the words. The baby is showing.

"The publicist is working on it, Bronwyn. The estate planners and lawyers all have red tape to get through. That's not just any baby in there. That's the only heir to our fortune.

That baby is going to be the richest child in the state, and we don't even know who the father is.

"We do know," I whispered.

"No. It isn't confirmed who the father is until the testing is done."

The conversation was getting old. If Dylan wasn't the father, then the baby was a true miracle – Dylan was the only man I'd been with for the past two years. But my parents couldn't handle the idea of a Laketownie being the father of their heir. If I had siblings, I'm pretty sure I would've been disowned, but since I was an only child, they had to figure out how they wanted to deal with this situation.

"I'm not a prisoner here. If I want to go to town to get a pizza, I'll go to town." It was childish, and I almost felt like stomping my foot but didn't.

"Pizza. Dear." The disapproval was palpable. "Your figure."

"It doesn't matter, Mom. My modeling career is over. You said it yourself."

Redness crept up my mom's neck and her shoulders slumped. "I shouldn't have said that. I was angry. I'm sure someone will hire you after…" she pointed to my stomach. Classic Joan, an apology wrapped in an insult.

I heard my father's voice echo in the foyer. "Who's there, Joanie?"

"It's Bron." My mom pulled me inside the cottage. "Don't upset your father."

I didn't know what she meant. Don't upset him how? By going to get a pizza. That seemed to be the worst thing in the world at the moment.

"Bron." My dad grinned and pulled me in for a hug. "Want a drink?"

Of course, it was four o'clock in the afternoon, my dad would have a two-finger pour of scotch, straight up waiting for him.

"Peter." My mom smacked him on the front of his polo shirt.

The smile disappeared from his face. "Right. Sorry, Bron. I forgot. Come, sit on the veranda with us and have a soda water or…"

"Soda water sounds good, Dad. But I was just heading into town."

Mom leaned in and didn't try to hide her whisper. "For a pizza."

"Pizza?" Dad's eyebrows raised. "I haven't had a pizza in a long time. I wonder if Potto's Pizza is still the place to go in town."

"It is," I smiled. "Lisa told me it's the best. Well, it's the only place in town – but they don't deliver."

My father grabbed my hand. "Come, let's have a drink. We'll get someone to bring us an old-fashioned Potto's Pizza." My dad had spent his summers in Laketown and lately seemed to be a sucker for nostalgia.

The screened-in veranda ran the width of the main cottage. White wicker furniture with nautical stripes arranged for conversations and sunset viewing was interspersed throughout. Ceiling fans spun lazily above us. The Yates' veranda had been featured in magazines and most of the cottages that were built in that era had verandas inspired by ours.

"Come, Bron. Have a seat." My father patted one of the cushions and took a seat on one of the chairs next to it. I smiled as I saw the glass of scotch, ready and waiting for him.

Mom sat beside Dad and one of their house staff, an older woman named Minerva appeared. The experienced staff knew how to monitor our actions and be seen when required.

"Mrs. Yates, would you like your cocktail now?" Minerva asked.

"Yes. And Minerva, could you get Bronwyn one too? And I'll take a glass of soda water."

Minerva nodded and disappeared into the house.

"Mom? A gin and tonic?" The wicker creaked as I rested into the back of the love seat.

My mom leaned in conspiratorially, "I'll drink yours. We can't have the staff talking."

I sighed. Why couldn't I have a baby shower and scream to the world that I had gotten knocked up? That the Yates fortune was going to go to a bastard baby with no father. I had lived a charmed life, I was well aware of that, but the past four months I'd felt the shame of my parents and was getting tired of it. "They're going to find out soon enough."

"Not if you're smart about it..." Her eyes darted behind me, and she eased into the chair beside my father.

Minerva had returned with the drinks and set them on the table along with nautical rope coasters.

"Cheers," Mom held up her glass and implored me with her eyes to play along in front of Minerva.

I picked up the glass with the lime on the side, squeezed it, and held it up as Minerva walked away. She had been with the family for years; I was pretty sure that she wouldn't gossip about our business. There weren't a lot of jobs in Laketown and working for our family was one of the most sought-after positions. At least, that's what I thought.

"Minerva." Dad took a sip and then called out.

She returned. "Is everything alright?"

"Can you order us a pizza?"

"Sir?"

My dad laughed. "Potto's Pizzeria, the biggest one you can get. Bronwyn, what would you like on it?"

I heard mom inhale beside me. If she could've shot fire from her eyes, she would've burned my father to a crisp. He was clueless and it made me smile.

"Pepperoni and cheese." I already felt guilty.

The skin beside his eyes crinkled as he smiled. "Just like when you were little." He nodded at Minerva. "A pepperoni and cheese pizza – get it here as fast as possible. Whatever it takes for my Bronwyn."

"Of course, Mr. Yates."

While we waited for the pizza my father regaled us with stories from the golf course. When I was younger, his play-by-play recollection of every hole on the course was the most boring thing I'd ever heard. Today, I was thankful for the useless banter. I nodded and smiled and added in a few comments about each hole.

"I'm playing at the Lake Casper Club tomorrow," he added at the end of his story.

I held my breath. *Calliope.* I had completely forgotten that my father's pride and joy was sitting at the marina - wounded. The Lake Casper Club was an island course. He was going to have to take a boat to get there and the missing showpiece from the boathouse would be obvious.

"That's cool, Dad. I heard the course is in good shape." I hoped that my voice wasn't as shaky as it sounded in my head. I had no idea what shape the course was in.

"We have had a lot of rain," he mused.

I had to spin the story, he was going to find out one way or another. "The marina guy…" I pretended not to remember Floyd's name. "Dropped by and picked up one of the boats. He said something about routine maintenance."

"White mustache?" Dad asked.

"Yeah, that's the one."

The screen door slid open, and we turned to see the house manager. I was thankful for the interruption, hoping it was the end of the *Calliope* discussion.

"I hear someone else was at the Lake Casper club today." Our house manager was one of the few Yates' family staff that knew about my baby. She had been in charge of coordinating the redesign of my bunkie to include a nursery and had insisted that the designers, a couple of local women, sign a nondisclosure agreement.

It all seemed so excessive. Growing up, I had wanted to be a famous model. Now, all I wanted was to be normal. What good was having all this fortune if I couldn't truly be me?

My mom turned to face me. "Were you at the club today?"

I took a sip of the soda water, letting it fizz in my throat before I answered her. "I met Tess and a few other friends for lunch."

The ice cubes rattled in my mom's glass as she polished off her gin and tonic. Minerva appeared out of nowhere to take the glass and soon returned with another duo of drinks for us.

"Bronwyn, you're going to have to get used to keeping a lower profile."

My dad crossed and uncrossed his legs, then cleared his throat. "Joan, this is something that has to be dealt with. We can't keep Brownyn locked up here while the lawyers figure out what to do."

My parents had been in the Bahamas for the last couple of months, so my dad and I hadn't had the chance to sit down and discuss the baby. It seemed a touch ironic that it was the person not in the Yates' lineage, my mom, who was most interested in protecting the fortune. My dad was the lone child of his generation, and after Joan had a terrible pregnancy with me, had disappointed his parents by only having a female heir.

But what's worse than a female heir?

A female heir who is pregnant with a bastard child.

My mom squeezed lime into her drink. "I just want what's best for Bronwyn."

I tried not to laugh. What we were doing was not, in any

way, what was best for me. My stomach growled and I wondered when the pizza was going to arrive.

"We will get it sorted out, Bron," my dad said. "It's just…" he hesitated and then continued, "complicated."

We were interrupted by the thwack of helicopter blades coming over the horizon, low and loud. "Pizza's here." My dad jumped from his seat.

"You sent the helicopter to get the pizza?" The thought had crossed my mind, but I'd dismissed it as absurd.

Dad shook his empty glass. "Well, none of us could drive. And Minerva had to stay and make the drinks."

"Dad," I was exasperated. "I could have driven into town."

His eyes flashed. "No, you couldn't."

There was usually a staff complement of at least ten anytime my grandparents were at the cottage, and even more when everyone was here. The unexpected arrival of my parents left us with a skeletal crew that currently consisted of Minerva, the house manager, no drivers, and a helicopter pilot.

While Dad went to meet the world's most expensive pizza delivery boy, a softer side of my mom showed up. "How are you feeling?"

"Well, I threw up today." Just the thought of my salmon salad lunch made me queasy all over again.

My mom nodded and patted my knee. "With you, my face broke out, I put on sixty pounds, and I was sick as a dog for two months straight."

Was my mom opening up to me? I felt uncomfortable. This was out of our wheelhouse. I put on a smile. "I have a lot to look forward to then."

My mom laughed. "Well, you're still beautiful, so maybe you're having a boy." I heard voices approaching and my dad reappeared wielding a giant pizza box and a smile. Minerva wasn't too far behind him with placemats, linen napkins, and a proper pizzeria pizza stand.

I felt like I had been transported back in time. Before I started modeling, and before my mom started worrying about getting old, we used to do fun stuff.

Minerva placed a slice on each of our plates and returned with a pitcher of lemonade, bottles of seltzer, and of course one more scotch, and one more gin and tonic. After she left, I turned to my mom and laughed. "You're going to feel those tomorrow."

She smiled. Her words were starting to get a bit slurred and she held up the glass. "I'm doing this for you, you know."

Her martyrdom was cute but made me angry. She wasn't hiding the fact that I was pregnant to help me. She was hiding it to help the family.

I took a bite of pizza and my eyes rolled as the cheesy deliciousness melted in my mouth. My dad folded his piece in half and groaned even louder than I did when he took a bite.

"I wonder if Potto's pizzeria was around when Granny was young?" I asked.

My dad finished chewing and scrunched his forehead. "I think Potto's opened when I was about five years old." He had just celebrated his 55th birthday, so that meant the pizza parlor was at least 50 years old.

My dad finished his slice and dabbed his mouth with his napkin. "Bronwyn, your mother and I love you. I know this has been hard on you, but we will figure it out, I promise. You're just going to have to be patient."

I smoothed the linen napkin over the skirt of my dress. "I know it's complicated, Dad. I wish it didn't have to be this way."

He cleared his throat. "Bronwyn, when I went to get the pizza, the house manager told me something disturbing."

Shit.

That could be one of two things. *Calliope* or Dylan.

"She said that someone dropped you off at the dock today." His tone was matter-of-fact.

My heart fell into my stomach and landed amongst the pizza. My thoughts churned and I wondered just how much the house manager saw.

I tried to brush it off. "It was a water taxi."

Dad narrowed his lips and stared at me. "Water taxi?" he asked doubtfully.

I took another bite of pizza and nodded. I didn't know what to say, and even though the pizza wasn't sitting well, it seemed easier to eat than to explain.

"Why didn't you take your boat?" My dad crossed his legs and folded his hands on his knee. My boat was a nice bowrider but showing up to the club in my boat would've been like arriving at a ball in a pickup truck.

The lie came out easily. "I went to lunch with Tess, in her boat, and she drank too much Prosecco."

My dad was quiet. The air hung heavy between us.

"You haven't seen that Moss boy, have you?"

Moss boy. He couldn't even bring himself to say his name.

I glanced into the cottage where the house manager was typing furiously on her phone. Had she seen Dylan kiss me on the end of the dock?

"He was driving the water taxi."

"Bronwyn," my mom gasped. "You were specifically told to stay away from him. He cannot know that he is the father."

I crossed my arms across my chest and winced at an unexpected pain. My breasts were feeling full, and my nipples were tender.

"Are you ready to admit that I haven't been lying? That Dylan--"

My dad interrupted, "The paternity test will confirm it."

I wanted to scream. We had been through this already. "Dad, I told you that it's him. There is no way it's anyone else."

"Well, Bronwyn. We know what you and your girlfriends get up to here in the summer when no one's around. And trust me, it would be better if it were one of the Lake Casper Club boys."

I set my plate on the table so hard it clattered. "For a minute, it felt like you were turning into a good dad."

"Do not speak to your father like that," Mom hissed.

I stood and put my hands on my hips. "Do not talk to him how Mom? He just all but called me a whore. His own daughter. We are hiding something from the father of my child. And while I get it, I don't like it."

"Oh, please," Mom muttered. "The only reason that boy would want to be involved is for the money."

My mind flashed to Dylan's smile and the way he carried me across the rocky gravel. He wasn't an opportunist. Sure, he liked to party and play hockey and drink beer, but he also cared about people. And even though he'd never said the words, I knew that he cared about me.

Probably because I cared about him.

"That's a pretty big assumption, Mom. And a shitty one."

My mom pushed the untouched pizza slice away from her. "You're sweet and you're young. Trust me, I know how the world works."

"Why is it so hard to believe that there's a man out there who likes me for me? That this child…" I smoothed my hand over the front of my belly, "could have an amazing father who honestly cares about what's best for his daughter." I glared at my father.

"You're out of line." Mom stood and pointed at me. "If you want to be a Yates, you will do what your father tells you to do, and right now, he's telling you to stay away from that boy. To keep that baby a secret until we tell you otherwise. Got it?"

I looked to my father, hoping that he would see just how crazy the whole situation was, and just how crazy his wife was behaving, but instead, he doubled down. He stood and pointed to the door. "Leave. Go to your bunkie and think about someone besides yourself for once. Think about the family."

I couldn't believe it. "You're sending me to my room?"

"It's hardly a room, Bronwyn. I'm sending you to the bunkie that just had a two hundred-thousand-dollar renovation to hide your mistake.

I had never felt so trapped, but I didn't know what to do. When my mom stood next to my father, the two of them a united front, I did what any spoiled child would do. I snatched the pizza box and stormed out.

I hadn't been a rebellious teenager. I hadn't slept around that summer. They were wrong about me, and they were wrong about Dylan.

SIX
DYLAN

WEDNESDAY MORNING PRACTICES were the worst. That's because they were our earliest, and I'm no morning person. I'd be happier if every practice was at midnight – a vampire league.

The guys were usually tired and the early morning practices a little quieter than the evening ones, but I could see that Tanner wasn't himself. He was a quiet guy, to begin with, but he hadn't said anything at all since he arrived at the rink. The defenseman, who was only eighteen but towered over the rest of the guys on the team, had been staring at the rubber mats on the floor.

"What's up, dude?" I sat down next to him on the bench while the rest of the team filed out of the dressing room and headed to the ice.

He inhaled deeply and then stood. "It's nothing."

I should've let it go. But there were two reasons I couldn't. One, I was selfish and wanted the team to play well. The big defenseman in front of me clearly had something on his mind, other than hockey. And two, I really cared about all the guys on the team. Every single one of them. Especially since that cocky bastard Gunnar Lockwood left.

"Dude." I glanced around to make sure all of the players had left. "There's something on your mind. I can see it."

Tanner tried to push past me, but I stepped in his way. "You're angry."

It was a statement.

"No shit. Mossy." At least he wasn't angry enough to call me by my real name. A nickname meant I hadn't thoroughly pissed him off yet.

"Good," I growled.

Tanner knitted his brow at me. "It's good that I just found out my girlfriend is cheating on me?"

He was an eighteen-year-old hockey star. He would get over it.

The door opened and our assistant coach, Leo stuck his head in. "You guys coming?"

"Yeah, Coach." Tanner slipped his mouthguard onto his teeth, determined to end the conversation.

"We're just going to be a minute, Coach." It still felt weird calling one of my former teammates Coach.

Leo looked between Tanner and me and nodded. "I'll tell Coach Covington you'll be out in a few minutes."

The door closed and Tanner took out his mouthguard. "What the hell, Dylan?"

There it was. My name. He was pissed.

"Where do you feel your anger?" I asked.

Tanner squinted at me and gave me a dirty look. "What?"

I slapped him on the chest. "Where is your anger?"

"I don't fucking know." He shook his head and tried to step around me. I sidestepped and stood in front of him and got in his face.

"Tell me."

I was the captain and except for one season, had been a

Laketown Otter for four years. This new guy knew his place on the roster and would never dream of talking back to me. Unless I pushed him, which is what I was doing.

"Tell you what, Dylan? I don't get the question. If you don't get out of my face, you're going to be the one getting the punch reserved for the asshole banging my girlfriend."

His dull eyes had turned fiery.

"What's his name?" I knew I was pushing it.

"Some rich prick named Robbie."

I picked up a puck from the bench and held it in front of Tanner's face. "Today. This puck is named Robbie." I shoved it into his glove. "Got it?"

The side of his lips turned up and I could see the lightbulb go off above his head. His eyes flickered as his anger transferred from me to the puck. "Send this puck through the fucking glass. Got it?"

I took a step back. Tanner tossed the puck into the air, caught it, and then with the arm of an American League pitcher, threw the puck at the concrete wall. I ducked reflexively as the puck ricocheted and landed on the bench. We stood for a moment admiring the black mark it left on the wall.

"Now scream," I ordered.

He didn't hesitate and let out a low baritone scream. I patted my chest with my glove and let out a guttural roar. The room vibrated with the sound and when we were done, both of us were panting. "Ready to play?" I asked.

Tanner stood taller, looked stronger, and his eyes were full of fire. Some guys swear that they need anger to play well. Based on what I've seen with my players, this is true for some of them, but especially Tanner. As Captain, it's my job to get the guys riled up.

Other guys need to Zen out. Gunnar Lockwood was the king of visualization, meditated before every game.

Me, I can play whenever, wherever no matter what I'm feeling. This is what I'm trying to teach these guys, as their captain. If they just fought with their girlfriend? I told them to use it. To bring it onto the ice and do something with it. If they were sad? Use it.

Some of my best games were in the days after my parents died. Back then the only way I could express myself was with my stick in my hand and my skates on the ice.

I kept an eye on Tanner throughout practice. My chest swelled like a big brother as he killed every drill in the practice. It felt good to be back on the ice. The rink was like a second home to me. The players, my family. The second I stepped through the door I was treated with respect.

I hadn't been able to relax since my run-in with Bronwyn. I tried not to feel used, but it was hard not to. The last time we saw each other had been hot, and she told me she couldn't wait to see me again. And then it was crickets. I just wished that she could've seen me in my Otters jersey instead of my dirty mechanic's shirt.

After a grueling round of suicide drills, Leo skidded to a stop next to me. "What did you do to the kid?"

I laughed. "I took him up to the stars and then brought him back down again."

Leo gave me a side glance and then smiled. "It worked."

"Thanks." I felt a sense of brotherly pride as we watched Tanner drill slapshot after slapshot into the net.

"What about you?" Leo rested his chin in the end of his stick.

I looked at him with my brow furrowed. "Me?"

Leo cleared his throat and then tapped his stick on the ice. "Yeah, you. Something's up."

This was news to me. I'd killed all the plays and put everything I had into the drills. What was Leo seeing that I wasn't?

I shrugged. "Maybe I'm dehydrated." As if to solidify my point, I took a bottle and squirted some electrolyte water into my mouth.

"Maybe." Leo nodded, but his eyes told me he didn't buy it. "Drink some more and get back to it." He skated away.

He was right. My body had been at the practice, but my mind hadn't. I should've taken Tanner's pep talk and used it on myself. There had to be some way I could get the image of that red dress whipping in the wind to stop replaying over and over in my mind.

WHEN I GOT HOME, a big black Mercedes SUV, one of the really expensive boxy ones, was parked in the driveway. The last time I had seen Bronwyn, she was driving a white Range Rover, but the Yates had a fleet of cars at every one of their places.

Was driving away an option? I checked my watch. I needed to get inside and get ready for work. I approached the SUV like I was approaching a car wreck, grimacing as I neared, waiting to see a flash of blond hair in the driver's seat. But as I reached the car, there wasn't even a shadow of a human being behind the tinted windows. I looked to the front door, which I left unlocked. A fact that she knew and had teased me about. Would she have the audacity to let herself into my house? And why was she there?

My hockey bag felt heavy on my shoulder. I tossed it onto the porch swing and stepped inside the house. I didn't announce my presence. It was my damn house after all. I heard the sound of pans crashing in the kitchen and then the whirr of the coffee grinder.

"What the hell?" It was too much. I kicked off my flip flops and stormed into the kitchen, ready to put that crazy woman in her place. Breaking and entering and making coffee?

I stopped in my tracks at the entryway to the kitchen and if I could've slapped myself in the face, I would have. It wasn't a crazy supermodel in my kitchen, it was my younger sister Jessie and her fiancé, one of my former teammates, Kane Fitzgerald.

"Dylan." Jessie smiled and paused the grinding of the coffee to give me a quick hug and then was back to the grinder. Caffeine was Jessie's drug of choice.

"Fitzy." I opened my arms and got a better hug from my former teammate.

I realized that my heart had been pounding, my body had chosen fight over flight, and now that the tension had released from my body, I slumped onto one of the wooden kitchen chairs. "What are you guys doing here?"

Jessie dumped the grounds into the coffee maker, sat down across from me and slid her hand into Kane's. Her diamond ring was one of the biggest I had ever seen, and I was happy for her. I could never give a woman a ring like that, but at least one of the Moss kids had made something of themselves.

"We both have a break from training, so we're staying at the cottage for a while," Kane explained. Like Bronwyn, Kane Fitzgerald had a family estate on Lake Casper, although Pine Hill, Fitzy's cottage, a gorgeous classic Laketown cottage looked like a shack compared to the Yates Estate.

I smiled. "Must be nice."

Jessie shot me a glare. "We're also meeting with the wedding planner and tasting cake at the Lake Casper Club."

"Right. Your wedding." I rolled my eyes and pretended as though I'd forgotten about it. It's all that she'd been able to talk about for the last six months. Jessie and Kane lived in the city, Kane played Center for the New York Thunder and

Jessie was on the national figure skating team and was training for the Olympics.

Jessie smacked me on the arm. "Don't be a jerk. Have you bought your suit yet?"

The money had been in my account for a month since Jessie sent it to me. I just hadn't gotten around to getting fitted for a suit that cost more than the beat-up dirt bike I rode to work. I wasn't in the wedding party, which was fine with me. Kane's National League buddies were all standing up for him. My job was more important anyway, I was walking my sister down the aisle. Something our dad would've done if he were still alive.

"I can just rent one, can't I?"

Kane laughed. "Dude, rental suits don't fit hockey players."

"Yeah, remember when you went to prom?" Jessie giggled. "Those socks…"

At 6'4, my suit had been at least four inches too short. I had improvised by finding the brightest, most obnoxious socks, they were yellow with angry-looking ninja cats. "I think I still have those socks." I pumped my eyebrows at her.

"Don't you dare with those ninja kitties," she laughed.

I leaned back in the chair as the smell of coffee filled the small kitchen. "What are you two doing here? Don't they stock coffee at Chez Fitzy?"

The glance between them was obvious and I sat a little straighter in the chair.

Jessie played with her cuticles, a sign that she was nervous. "We wanted to talk to you about Sidney."

"Sidney?"

"Oh, my God, Dylan." Jessie groaned. "I knew it." She rolled her eyes and looked at Kane.

"What?" I was thoroughly confused.

Jessie slipped her hand back into Kane's. "Sidney, the

figure skater that you agreed to bring to the wedding as your date when we were at the pub by our condo."

"What?" This was news to me.

The memory was hazy at best. The last time I had been in the city to visit Jessie we had gone to a dive bar with her figure skater friends. All of them were getting hit on, except one girl. She wasn't ugly, but she wasn't pretty either – and if I recall, didn't really have anything to talk about except edge control and nut butters she was allergic to. Getting wasted and going home with strange women had been my thing for a few years, but since I'd met Bronwyn, there hadn't been a woman who had caught my eye, no matter how many empty beer steins ended up in front of me.

"I was just being nice to her." I groaned. "There was no talk of a wedding. If there was, I clearly forgot about it."

The coffee machine sputtered as it finished. Jessie got up and took three mugs out of the cupboard. "Well, she didn't."

"Jess," I sighed. "That was months ago."

Jessie added cream to my coffee and sugar to Kane's and stirred as she spoke, the spoon clanking against the ceramic mugs. "Dylan." My younger sister had perfected her disappointed in me look years earlier and it was clear she hadn't forgotten it. "You sat with her all night."

"Jess. It's coming back to me now, but I don't ever recall asking her to go to your wedding as my date. I don't get that drunk anymore."

She raised her eyebrows as if she didn't believe me. "Well, you didn't ask her. She asked you."

"What?" I couldn't screw my forehead up any tighter. "I remember talking about almond butter, cashew butter, oh and heaven forbid – peanut butter, and then some of the different rinks we've skated in, but seriously, Jessie. I'm sorry. I don't remember agreeing to take your friend who I have zero chemistry with to your wedding. I didn't think that I even needed a date."

I took a sip of my coffee hoping that the caffeine would jolt a memory into my brain. "You came to the table when we were talking about the new barn that had just opened in Carstead."

"You were talking about a barn. Like a skating rink." Jessie trained her eyes on mine.

I forgot that figure skaters didn't use our slang. "Yeah, a barn. Like an arena, you know, with ice."

Jessie squeezed her eyes shut and her nostrils flared. "You do realize that Kane and I are getting married in a barn. An actual barn, with no ice."

"Ohhhhh." It was starting to make sense. "So when she asked if I wanted to go to the barn with her, she wasn't asking me to test drive the new ice."

Jessie crossed her arms. "Nope."

"Shit," I muttered.

"Shit is right. Can you just suck it up and go with her?"

"What?" I set my mug on the table harder than I expected and coffee sloshed on my thumb. I wiped it off on the leg of my jeans. "No."

"Kane? Can you help me out with this?" Jessie said.

Kane, who I'd forgotten was in the room watching our brother and sister scrap was leaning back in the kitchen chair with an amused look on his face. He held up his hands, "You're on your own with this one. But…" he sighed and leaned his elbows on the table. "She's going to be at the wedding anyway, so you're going to need a good excuse if you're going to get out of this one, brother."

I nodded my head while I ran simultaneous scenarios through my head, one that included attending in disguise.

"And not going to your sister's wedding is not an option," Kane laughed but there was a serious undertone to his voice.

My brain was going a million miles an hour. I could be nice and take the most boring girl in the world to one of the best parties of the year. She was Jessie's teammate. I couldn't just ghost her – especially if she was going to be there anyway. What excuse could get me out of this?

"What's her number?" I slid my phone across the table to Jessie. "I'll take care of it."

Jessie put the girl's number in my phone, Sidney. I had forgotten her name already.

"So, you're taking her?"

"No." I put the phone in the pocket of my shirt. "I'm going to tell her that there was a misunderstanding about the barn. You know, be honest."

"Dyl," Jessie chided.

She wasn't going to let it go. "And that I already have a date for the wedding."

Kane and Jessie's eyebrows rose in unison.

"That second part is a lie." Jessie waggled her finger at me.

"No," I smiled. "It's true. I have a date for your wedding."

Jessie looked dubious. "Who?"

"A friend." Her name came out of my mouth before I formulated how to make it happen. "Bronwyn Yates."

Kane choked on his coffee and pounded his chest with his fist. Jessie rubbed his arm and looked at me with her eyes narrowed. "Bronwyn Yates is going to our wedding as your..." She pointed at my coffee-stained jeans, "Dylan Moss's date."

"Yep," I grinned and finished my coffee.

My heart started to pound for two reasons. One, the idea of walking into the wedding with Bronwyn on my arm, and two, the way I'd have to get her to do it.

SEVEN
BRONWYN

A soft knock on the door, followed by the creak of the bedsprings woke me from yet another one of my crazy pregnancy dreams. My hair was stuck to my neck, and I groaned as I rolled and reached for the bottle of artesian spring water I'd almost finished before I fell asleep reading. The *Shopoholic,* sat open to the same page I'd been reading for the past three nights.

"Morning, Miss Lisa." I opened the bedroom door a crack and greeted my housekeeper. I could hear her rustling around in the kitchen and the tick of the gas range as she put the kettle on to boil.

"Good morning, Miss Bronwyn," she replied. When Lisa first started working for me, I had been quick to correct her when she called me Miss Yates, but we found a compromise and referred to each of each other as Miss. I liked it and I'm pretty sure that Lisa liked it too. "I picked up some scones from the bakery. Do you want one while they're still warm?"

At the height of my modeling career, I wouldn't have even dared to smell carbs, let alone eat baked goods from the iconic Laketown bakeshop, but my stomach growled, and they seemed like one of the few breakfast items that I'd be able to keep down. First pizza, then scones? Who was I?

"No yoga this morning?" Lisa asked as I slid onto the barstool in my silk robe and slippers.

"Maybe in a little while." I stretched my hands above my head, which was the most yoga-like thing I'd done in a week. Sleep just seemed more important than following my grueling early morning workout routine. Lisa set a cup of steaming tea and the scone in front of me, but after one bite the smell of the blueberries made me nauseous. I slid the plate away and took a couple of deep breaths and a sip of tea.

"Everything alright, Miss Bronwyn?" Lisa looked at me with concern in her eyes.

"It's fine," I smiled. "I just need a minute."

Lisa nodded. "My friend Morgan had awful morning sickness, but my sister Jennifer couldn't stop eating. Everyone is different," she shrugged.

I knew that she was trying to make me feel better. "Wait, your sister – your younger sister had a baby?" At twenty-three, I felt too young to have a baby. Lisa was still in high school. "

"Last year."

"Wow." I didn't mean to say it out loud.

Lisa looked at me over her glasses. "I know what you're thinking, but it's kind of normal here."

I nodded, embarrassed that Lisa had caught me being judgmental. "You must be one cool aunt." I sipped my tea, hoping my attempt to lighten the conversation had worked.

"Totally," she laughed. "And Miss Bronwyn, my sister is happy with her choice."

"Of course." I looked into my mug. Was I projecting my embarrassment onto Lisa's sister? "I'm sure I will be happy too."

The pity flashed in her eyes quickly. "I know you will be."

"Thanks, Lisa." The nauseous feeling had passed. I finished the scone in three bites and eyed the cardboard box on the counter. "Are there any more in there?"

"You betcha," she grinned. "And an éclair, if you're feeling wild and crazy."

"Whoa, Nelly." I laughed and held my hands up in front of me. But I was already imagining the squish of the cream in my mouth.

My phone buzzed on the counter, and I glanced at the screen. Lake Casper Marine.

"Shit," I muttered through a mouthful of scone. "Hey, Lisa, has my dad gone to the boathouse yet?"

"I don't think so." Lisa started the dishwasher and was gathering up the clothes that I'd strewn across the living room while trying to find an outfit to wear to brunch the day before. "Your parents left in the helicopter this morning before I got here. You didn't hear it?"

I shook my head, but that explained the stampede of bison that had been about to trample me in my dream. "Do you know when they're coming back?" The house manager had a better handle on my parents' location than I did most of the time, and most of the staff did too.

"Your mom said something about the Vail house."

I smiled and felt a sense of relief wash over me. My parents went to the Vail house whenever my mom was getting plastic surgery done – that meant I had at least a week, but most likely two before they would be back in Laketown. Even though it was totally obvious that my mom got work done, she still liked to hide until the puffiness faded and the stitches were removed. "What about the house manager? Has she been down to the boathouse?"

Lisa scrunched up her forehead and I knew that a question was on the tip of her tongue, but I was still her boss, and she knew better than to interrogate me. "No, she's been preparing the staff for the arrival of your grandmother."

Double shit. If my dad found out that I'd taken *Calliope* out and ruined her, he'd be pissed, but my grandmother – that was worse than the illegitimate baby. If it wasn't quite disowning territory, it was definitely cold shoulder, slash a few zeroes off the inheritance territory. I rushed into the bedroom and pulled on a pair of black yoga pants and a black T-shirt and I swept my hair up into a loose bun. Together with the gold chain on my Chanel bag, my outfit looked mostly pulled together. I typically wouldn't go out in public in such a rush, but I had to get to the marina before the house manager found out about the boat. I didn't know how, but I had to fix this mess. I turned to the side and smoothed my hand over my T-shirt. I could tell that my stomach wasn't flat and hard, but to an onlooker, it might look like I had just eaten a big breakfast. I hoped.

"Is everything alright?" Lisa asked.

I had gone from lethargic to warp speed in a matter of seconds. "It will be," I said to the mirror. More to myself than to Lisa. "I'm taking my boat out. I'll be back soon."

"Miss Bronwyn?" Lisa paused as she wiped the crumbs from my scone off the island. "Do you want me to come with you?"

It was an odd question, but then again, I was pregnant and heading out onto the lake on my own. "I'll be fine, Lisa. I've been driving boats since I could walk."

She nodded. "Don't forget your earrings, I left them on the ledge in the bathroom.

I never left home without my Tahitian pearls, and I reached up to feel the emptiness in my ear, surprised that I hadn't noticed. Was this pregnancy brain? Or, was I just worried about the boat – or could it have something to do with the fact that I hadn't been able to go more than ten minutes without thinking of Dylan?

The earrings were exactly where Lisa had placed them. With the thought of potentially running into Dylan, I swiped on my trademark red lipstick. Leaning against the counter I took a deep breath, stared at my reflection for a second, and then took off for the boathouse at a pace that could rival an Olympic speed-walker.

When I left the dock at the cottage, the mist had hung heavily over the lake, the dampness clinging to my clothes and the humidity wreaking havoc on my ballerina bun, but by the time I got to the marina, the sun had risen above the horizon and burned off the mist. The lake was like a mirror, the treeline reflected perfectly in its surface. There were two reasons that Lake Casper and Laketown were so popular. It was the place to be for the elite from all over the country; but for those who had been there from the beginning, before the arrival of the oyster bars and golf courses, it was the sheer beauty – the contrast of the green pines and the deep clear lakes. That's what had drawn the Yates family there all those years ago, to escape the heat from the city.

The young man, Sam from the day before, was awaiting my arrival at the dock. He tied the lines and offered me his hand. "Good morning, Miss Yates." He smiled, but his lips held a slight tremble. I squeezed his hand and gave him a warm smile. Being a supermodel, I was used to men being flustered around me. This young boy was a lot more composed than some of the grown men who had crossed my path.

"Do you need your boat fueled up?" His voice cracked as I released his hand.

"No, Sam. I'm here to see Floyd."

The young man pulled the radio from his belt and

pointed to the building with its antennae. I'll let him know you're here."

"Thank you." I slipped a hundred from my purse and handed it to him.

He shook his head. "No ma'am. No need for that. This is my job."

He was adorable. I hoped that my son would grow up to be as well-mannered as this dock boy.

My son.

Why did that thought come to me? I hadn't wanted to know whether it was a boy or a girl. Somehow that seemed to make everything all that more real. But a son. I touched my belly and knew, that I was nurturing a son – and it felt right.

When I reached the marina, I realized that I had been walking with my hand on my stomach. An unconscious and dead giveaway of either a baby or constipation – neither was good for Bronwyn Yates, especially if the paparazzi were around.

It wasn't Floyd who greeted me at the garage bay door, it was the white-haired lady, Thelma, who I assumed was either his sister or his wife. "Miss Yates." Her smile was warm, and she reminded me of Mrs. Claus. Her hands were the softest I'd ever felt and after she shook my hand, my own felt like they'd had their own treatment. The smell of her moisturizer was shea butter and another smell I couldn't quite place.

"Floyd will be in shortly," she smiled. "Would you like a cup of coffee, dear?"

I almost said yes, the adrenaline from the rush to get to the marina just in case they called the house manager instead of me, had worn off and suddenly I felt exhausted.

"No, thank you." I smiled. "But I could go for a bottle of water if you've got one." Thelma handed me a bottle of water and left me waiting in the plastic chair outside Floyd's dark office. The boat I'd been admiring the day before sat in the bay and as the early morning sunshine poured in through the windows. It was as if Mother Nature had her very own spotlight and was showing off the craftsmanship. I rubbed my hands together and made a mental note to ask Thelma what moisturizer she used on her hands.

I glanced at my phone to check the time and sighing, I flipped through a five-year-old tabloid magazine, and then checked my phone again. Beyond the windows in the small waiting room, I could see activity in the large bays; mechanics milling around and shouting to each other. Dylan was nowhere to be seen, and I racked my brain trying to remember if he ever told me what days of the week he worked. Throughout our time together, we didn't talk about work. It was nice. He didn't care what runways I'd walked, and I didn't care that he fixed boats for a living. The conversations had been a surprise to me – there was a depth to Dylan I'd never experienced with another man. The nauseous feeling from earlier returned and the small white waiting room with the terrible-smelling coffee pot seemed to close in on me.

One more nonchalant check through the window ensured that the tallest, best-looking mechanic wasn't anywhere to be seen, so I took the opportunity to step out of the waiting room, and into the somewhat better smelling, but not by much, garage bay. The wooden boat shone, and I couldn't stop myself from reaching out to touch it again. Yesterday it had felt like silk, and I wondered if my eyes were playing tricks on me, but today it looked shinier, brighter, smoother. I ran my finger along the side and yes, it was smoother. My reflection shone back at me as I trailed my fingertips along the gunwale. I jerked my hand back when the smoothness gave way to stickiness.

"Oh no," I whispered and stepped back. I glanced behind me to see if anyone had seen me touching the boat, but everyone seemed absorbed in their jobs. Crouching down, the very clear smudge with the obvious swirls of my finger-print was obvious. "Shit," I muttered. I should've known better. Just like touching a tacky manicure twice – I touched it again and ruined everything.

"Stop!" A voice boomed from behind me, and I jerked my hand to my chest. A tool fell to the ground in a clatter and all of a sudden, every eye in the garage was on me, as I held my Varathane-sticky finger to my chest with my other hand.

Dylan dropped his hockey bag on the concrete floor with a thud and jogged to the side of the boat. His gaze immediately honed in on the smudge. He inhaled sharply and crouched so his eyes were level with the print. His eyes remained closed for longer than a blink.

"I'm sorry, Dylan," I whispered. "I didn't know it was wet."

His eyes flitted open and he turned to face me. "You couldn't tell it was wet?" His eyes were dark pools and if there was emotion in them, I couldn't see it. He shook his head. "It's fine." He brushed past me and disappeared into Floyd's office. I slipped back into the waiting room, embarrassed that I'd ruined the boat's varnish. I didn't know why Dylan would care, but the disappointment in his eyes was the same as when the hockey team from Montreal won the cup. It had taken one serious blow job to cheer him up on that night. We had watched the game together, curled up on the overstuffed sofa in the bunkie, while rain poured on the steel roof. It was one of my favorite memories of us together. But today, something told me that he needed something more than a BJ to cheer him up.

Floyd still hadn't arrived, and I peered through the window to see Dylan on the phone at Floyd's desk. When he hung up, I knocked on the door and opened it wide enough to stick my head in. "I'm really sorry, Dylan. I'll pay for the boat to get re-shellacked, or whatever it's called.

"Money can't fix everything, Bronwyn." I could barely hear his voice, but his comment screamed at me.

"I know." I stepped into the office and closed the door behind me. "But I don't know what else to offer."

His eyes softened. "Your Varathaning skills aren't up to the task?"

The sparkle in his eye was back and with it, my confidence. "I'm a fast learner. And how different can it be from painting nails?" I wiggled my perfect manicure at him. Since I'd been at the cottage, I'd done the touch-ups myself.

He rolled his eyes and then looked at me seriously. "What are you doing here so early?"

I took this as an invitation to stay and perched on one of the chairs opposite Floyd's desk. "I wanted to talk to Floyd about *Calliope*."

He nodded and the purse of his lips told me he had news – and it wasn't good. "I just spoke with him."

"And?" I leaned forward. His hair was wet, and his cheeks were flushed and with the intensity of his gaze, and my cheeks soon matched his. He steepled his fingertips together and pumped his eyebrows twice before his trademark smirk appeared on his full lips, sending my heart racing for two reasons – one, the obvious – this flirtation was turning me on, and two, the suspense of the boat's fate.

"Enough with the drama, Moss. What's going on with the boat? Is my grandmother going to disown me?" I said it with a smile on my face but was only partially joking.

He eased back in the chair, his hands still steepled like a mafia boss from an eighties' movie. "How much is it worth to you to keep your little outing a secret?"

"A secret?"

"Is there an echo in here?"

"Are you trying to blackmail me, Dylan Moss?" It had never been about the money with him, and the Cheshire cat smile on his face told me that the threat wasn't a serious one.

He picked up the phone and cradled it between his shoulder and ear. "So, I can call your —what is it you call her? — your house manager, and tell her that *Calliope* needs an engine rebuild because she was stolen by a couple of supermodels?"

"No." I shot to my feet and jabbed at the button to ensure the phone wasn't connected. "That's why I came in. I don't want anyone to find out about this. I'll deal with it. My parents don't even know that she's missing... yet."

He set the earpiece to the phone back on the main part. "Let me get this straight. You're hoping to get the boat fixed, on the down-low, and get her back to your Estate without your family finding out." He sounded dubious.

"That's the plan." I crossed my arms across my chest.

"Well, then if that's what you need, I think I can help."

Relief washed over me, and I leaned into the backrest of the chair, not worrying about the slouchy posture. "Thank you."

He leaned forward and this time it was him who crossed his arms. "*Calliope* needs a rebuild. Luckily, I have exactly the parts you need."

I remembered Dylan talking about his dad's storage unit filled with antique boat parts. "Your dad's?"

"You remember that?"

"Vaguely." I tilted my head, trying to act like I hadn't just recalled an insignificant post-orgasm detail he'd shared with me over a year ago.

"We can probably get everything done in three or four days if it all goes to plan."

Three days. It could work.

"I will tell your house manager it's routine maintenance. No one will ever know the difference."

"Dylan." I stood and rushed behind the desk to hug him, but he held out his hand to stop me.

"As I said, it's going to cost you."

"Anything," I agreed hoping it wasn't a number so outrageous that one of the accountants would notice and question it.

He stood and stepped close to me. Uncomfortably close. Close enough that I could smell the fresh shampoo on his hair. I could feel the heat from his chest on mine, even though we weren't touching. Then he moved closer. Close enough that if he'd had a hard-on, the front of his mechanic's pants would've brushed the front of my yoga pants. "Was he going to ask for a sexual favor for payment?" My cheeks flushed with the notion. He'd already had me every way possible, but payment for sex? I wasn't a prostitute.

He kept his eyes trained on mine then slid something into my hand before stepping away. The intense heat, the energy between us, broke like the humidity after a thunderstorm. Dylan sat in Floyd's cushy leather chair and leaned back.

"What's this?" I turned over the envelope in my hand. It was heavy white card stock.

He jutted his chin at it. "Open it."

I pulled out an embossed cream-colored card and was instantly confused. "It's a wedding invitation." I looked a little closer and recognized both of the names of the bride and groom. "Your sister's getting married?"

He nodded. "Yep."

I turned the card over to see if I was missing something.

He took the card from my hand and held up a pen. "And I need a plus one."

EIGHT

DYLAN

THE CRISP AIR inside the arena always makes me forget about the outside world. It's as though stepping inside McManus Place, the whole rest of the world, and my problems, don't exist. The summer practice season was always a bit more laid back than the rest of the year, but we were prepping for the annual exhibition game. This was going to be my fourth as an Otter, and my stomach didn't have the same jumble of nerves that it has had in the past.

"Did you hear?" Jasper, one of the rookies was tightening his skates.

I dropped my hockey bag on the floor and sat beside him. "Hear what?"

"They're changing the exhibition game."

"How?" The annual Otters versus the pros was the highlight of the summer for most of the Laketown residents. It always sold out in minutes and everyone in town was in the stands.

"I'm not sure. But I think the coach is going to tell us."

I shook my head but didn't go as far as rolling my eyes. Small town gossip – at it again. "Don't listen to rumors, kid."

I got undressed and pulled on the bottom half of my practice gear and shrugged into my chest and shoulder protector. "Don't fix what ain't broke." It was a saying Floyd used all the time at work – for a reason: it made sense. The exhibition game was the perfect end to the summer and had made more than one Otter a national league player. The scouts were always in the crowd.

Coach Covington and Leo walked into the room and the silence was deafening as all the players stopped talking and stared at them. "They better not cancel it," Jasper whispered under his breath.

I shot a *shut the fuck up* look at Jasper and noticed three distinct blotches on his neck – hickeys. I couldn't help myself. Coach and Leo were discussing something by the play board and the room had filled with the din of conversation, but the players were keeping a close eye on the white-board. My hockey jersey hung in my cubby, and I grabbed it, but before I put it on, I flicked Jasper's neck.

"Ow. Fuck, dude." He rubbed at his neck.

I laughed. "Were the vampires out last night?"

The guy beside me, one of the veterans, Mike Ryan laughed. "I heard that he was attacked by two vamps."

"Vamps or tramps?" Tanner snarked.

I rolled my eyes. "Grow up, Tanner."

Mike flicked Jasper's neck on the other side. "Yeah, grow up, Tanner."

The camaraderie of the team was one of the things that drew me back to hockey. There had been a few rough years just after my parents died that I had chosen booze over play-ing, but Coach Covington had been the one to pick me up before I fell completely to the ground. Hockey saved my life and now my team was my family. And what do you do to your little brother? Torment him.

"Watch out," I whispered to Jasper. "The new puck bunnies have got a little bite."

"You're just jealous," Jasper grinned.

I wasn't. I had a date to a wedding with a supermodel. It was a coerced date, perhaps even blackmail, but Bronwyn was something I'd always wanted. A real woman.

"Be careful, buddy." I shoved his shoulder and put on my sweater. "Don't let them get territorial."

Jasper shrugged. "I know what I'm doing."

Mike, Tanner, and I all burst into laughter. "Rookies." Mike shook his head. "You'll have to learn the hard way."

Jasper's face got a little red under the stubble on his chin. "Speaking of weird marks. Dude, what's that on your back?"

The back of my sweater had gotten stuck on my chest protector, and I craned my neck to see what he was talking about.

"You look like you got punched by a bear." He pointed to my lower back and as I rubbed the spot with my hand, knew what it was. Oil. I had spent twenty minutes after work trying to scrub the oil from my nails – even with the latex mechanics gloves, I still walked out of the marina with filthy hands and had spent the day on my back under the stern of *Calliope*.

I tugged my shirt into place. "It's nothing." I wasn't exactly embarrassed, unlike Tanner, there were other guys on the team that had to work. I wasn't lucky enough to live at my family's cottage as Tanner did and play hockey all the time. For a lot of those guys, they treated getting into the National League like a full-time job. Me? I just loved playing hockey. Besides, no scout was interested in a player with a reputation for being a wild card. Plus, my hiatus from the game had taken me completely off their radar. Did it bother me? Kind of. As a kid, like every other kid in Laketown, I'd wanted to be a hometown hero, a hockey star, but that dream got lost when my mom and dad died. When I realized it wasn't the town that I wanted to be proud of me, it was them. At least, my sister had done something for herself. She was heading for the medal podium at the Olympics, and she was marrying one of the best guys I'd ever known.

Me? I had grease on my back and had to bribe a woman to be my date.

Coach Covington waved me over to the playboard. "Dylan, we want you to announce your team."

"Coach?" My brow furrowed so hard my eyes squinted. "What announcement?"

Coach and Leo shot each other a glance. "I'm surprised you haven't heard," he said. "Let's step into the hall."

Every eye in the room was on me as I followed the Coach and the assistant into the hallway. "You really haven't heard?" Leo gave me a dubious look and crossed his arms.

"Come on, guys. No. I haven't heard." I was starting to get pissed off. "When I'm not at practice, I'm at work, and when I'm not working, I'm working on my boat. And unlike the rest of this town, she isn't much of a gossiper."

Leo uncrossed his arms, but Coach crossed his. "Mind your tone, son. You might be the captain of this team, but we are still your coaches."

"Sorry, Coach." I shuffled my skates on the rubberized flooring of the hallway. "What's the big news and what do you want me to tell the team?"

"Leo." Coach gave a nod to his assistant.

Leo smiled. "The annual exhibition game is going to be a series."

"That's cool." A series was cool but didn't seem to merit the huge buildup. "How many games?"

Leo grinned. "It depends on how well we do. It's going to be a round-robin with eight teams."

"Eight teams? What about the pros? That's the big draw."

The exhibition game was a fun event for the local townspeople, they got to see the superstars in the Laketown Barn. Plus, if an Otter could shine in the exhibition game, playing against the National League guys, it seriously upped his chances of getting drafted.

Leo rubbed his hands together. "You really didn't hear?"

"Obviously, Leo. The guys, I don't think they're going to be too happy about this. We're top in the league, and one more series against the Northern professional guys, I mean, why?" I leaned against the wall and crossed my arms. No wonder they wanted me to break the news to the team. It was terrible.

"It's not Northern professional. The Otters are going to be in the first Laketown Summer Playoff Series against national league teams. McManus put this together. He's got huge sponsors, and it's going to be televised across the country."

"Hooooooly shiiiiiiit!" Everything was starting to make a lot more sense. "Why us?"

Coach smiled. "You said it yourself. We're the top team in the league. Only a few national league teams wanted to participate and there was space for one more. Not to mention that McManus is organizing the whole thing, and he happens to own this team."

My heart started to pound against my chest. This was like the exhibition game on steroids, but we didn't stand a chance. "Are you sure it's a good idea, Coach? I mean, we won't make it past the first round."

Coach's hand felt heavy on my shoulder pad. "Dylan, first of all, that's not the right attitude."

I sighed. "I know. I'm just nervous for us."

"Let me ask you a question. What have those national guys been doing all summer? I know that you've been to some parties with them."

I raised my eyebrow at Leo. He knew that I'd taken my foot off the gas when it came to the party scene, but I guess Coach still thought I was spending my weekends getting loaded and swimming naked with puck bunnies. "They've been at their cottages?" I wasn't sure what answer Coach was looking for.

"And, what else?"

"Golfing?"

"What else?"

I shrugged. "I don't know what answer you're looking for Coach. As far as I know, they party, drive around in their boats, and golf. That's it."

He smiled and nodded. "And what have you guys been doing?"

I let out a little laugh. "Practicing." I could see what he was getting at.

"Practicing and working out. You guys have a shot." Coach slapped the back of his clipboard.

I paused with my hand on the dressing room door handle and noticed that it was shaking. This was big fucking news.

"But, Dylan." Coach stopped me before I could pull open the door, "Don't tell them until after practice. This anticipation." He grinned. "It's good for them."

"Roger that, Coach." I nodded. Like me, Coach had been through a rough patch as well. It was good to see him with his head back in the game. He was one of the best in the league and we were lucky to have him.

I was lucky to have him.

STEAM HUNG HEAVILY in the dressing room as the players finished their showers. Everyone kept looking at me, waiting for me to stand up and confirm the rumors that they'd already heard. When the last guy, Jasper, was out of the shower I stood and picked up my bag. "See you guys later." I pretended to leave. I was immediately pelted with a bunch of gloves and even some pucks.

"Come on Dylan," Mike groaned, a puck waiting to be lobbed held in his left hand.

I turned and dropped my bag dramatically on the floor. "Alright, guys." I spread my arms wide like wings, "Are you ready for the greatest news you've ever had in your entire life?"

Mike threw the puck. "On with the show, ringmaster."

I caught the puck, tossed it into the air, spun, and caught it behind my back. I thought it was funny, but I could see a few of the guys glancing at each other, and their technical watches. I set the puck on the bench. "There is no exhibition game this year."

"What?" A collective murmur spread through the room.

I had tortured them enough. "There are going to be THREE. It's a round-robin and all of the other teams are from the National League. It's the biggest hockey event Lake-town has ever seen."

It took a second for the news to register and then the room shook as my teammates jumped to their feet. Some cheered, some roared, and some hugged. Jasper approached and pulled me aside.

"You said three games? But it's a round-robin."

"That's right, Rookie." I slapped him on the back. "We're playing in all three rounds because we're winning this fucking thing," I said loud enough for the whole team to hear. The nervousness I'd felt earlier was completely gone. We were a talented team, and Coach was right, we had a real shot. We just needed to believe it. As the captain, it was my job to make my team believe that we could beat three different National League Teams.

The thunder in the room got louder. The guys were pumped. It was my job to make sure they stayed that way.

SOMEONE CALLED my phone twice as I drove home from practice. But after working on my boat project and then working a full day at the marina, then practicing, I was spent and didn't answer. All I wanted to do was go home, turn on the tv, and fall asleep with a pizza box on my chest. I grabbed my jacket and hockey bag and headed into the house and my phone rang again. Multiple calls in a row were usually not a good thing and I fumbled with my jacket to find my phone.

It was Jessie. I took a deep breath and answered.

"Why aren't you answering your phone?" Her voice sounded anxious, and I immediately felt bad. After my rough patch, where I'd spend days drinking and not talking to anyone, I promised Jessie that I would never disappear on her again.

"I was driving and wanted to be safe." She couldn't argue with that. "I just walked in the door, what's up?"

"We're having a few friends over for dinner and want you to come."

"Sorry, I have plans." I tossed the keys to the car on the table and kicked off my flip-flops. The fridge was always fully stocked with cans of sparkling water, and I cracked one open."

"That better be water." Her voice was stern on the line.

I knew that she was coming from a place of love, but it had been over two years and I still hadn't slipped back into the surly drunk jerk that had gotten kicked off the Otters. I wanted to snap at her, but it felt very nice to know that someone cared. Mom was gone and Jessie, my younger sister had stepped into her role.

"The finest sparkling water from Delaware." I read the can and laughed.

"What are your plans? Watching hockey and falling asleep on the sofa?"

She knew me too well.

"No." I shifted the phone to the other ear so I could pre-heat the oven. "I'm eating pizza too."

"I thought so." She sounded triumphant and I didn't know why.

"What does that mean?"

Her laugh was light on the other end of the phone, and I could hear the sound of people talking and cupboards banging in the background. "Get over here. Kane's got the outdoor pizza oven stoked and a huge projection screen set up on the boathouse to watch some hockey hits and fights and stuff."

"Wood-fired pizza?" The frozen pizza clunked against the side of the box as I turned it over to read the instructions. "And Rock 'Em Sock 'Em on a big screen?"

"Yeah, that's what it's called. Now get over here."

She didn't give me the chance to say no, but suddenly my house felt lonely, and all of the pepperoni pieces had fallen to one side of my crappy grocery store dinner. I turned off the oven and put on my Otters' baseball hat. I didn't know who was going to be at Jessie's, but just in case Sidney was there, I needed to make my wedding date story a little more real. At least that's what I told myself as I scrolled through my phone to find Bronwyn's number. And, before I realized what a bad idea it was, the phone was ringing.

NINE
BRONWYN

IN THE PHOTOGRAPHY WORLD, they called that time the Golden hour. Why? My best guess was because anybody could look like a model in the golden hue from the setting sun. Everything in my bunkie had a warm glow. For the first time in weeks, I opened the door to the third bedroom. The blinds were closed, as they always were, for privacy and to keep prying eyes from seeing that my third bedroom had been turned into a nursery.

THERE WAS NO BABY SHOWER, all of the gifts matched perfectly and were exactly to my taste. I hadn't had any fun games where friends, melted chocolate bars into diapers and made me guess which chocolate bars they were, and part of me told me I didn't care. Those things were stupid, but keeping this baby a secret had been hard. I slid my hand to my belly, and as the baby grew, things in my life were only going to get harder.

My housekeeper, Lisa, had left me a jar of iced tea and I poured myself a glass and headed down to the dock. The staff had all gone back to the Yates' staff housing complex, which was a 20-minute walk away. It was a ghost town, and I loved it.

The glass of iced tea was sweating. Even in the early evening, it was still over eighty degrees. I had planned to watch the sunset sink behind the horizon, but dark black clouds started to appear, and I wasn't ready to get my yellow silk dress completely soaked.

Back in the bunkie, I saw that I had missed a call from Dylan. What could he want?

I wondered briefly but didn't call him back. He hadn't left a message, so it couldn't have been that important. My phone rang again, and my heart leaped into my throat. But when I looked at the screen it wasn't Dylan, it was Tess.

I hesitated, but seeing as Tess was one of my few friends in Laketown, and I was feeling a little lonely, I picked it up.

"Hello, Tess." I put on a bright voice.

"Bronwyn." Her voice was slurring and I could hear loud music in the background. She was either at Valerock or out at the island club.

"We're coming to get you," she shouted.

"Get me? Where are you?"

"We're out on Tad's boat, but we're going to go to Valerock for a sunset cruise and some cocktails. We'll be at your dock in 10 minutes."

I was lonely, but somehow, I knew that hanging out with Tess and the popped collar crowd at Valerock wasn't going to help. "Tess, I'm beat. I'm going to pass on Valerock tonight."

Tess must have thought she was whispering. "See, I told you she wouldn't come. She's totally fucking lame now."

Well, at least she'd noticed that I wasn't partying much anymore.

Tess put on a fake sad tone. "We are all going to miss you so much."

"Next time," I singsonged, then hung up the phone before my supposed best friend could say anything more.

I dropped the phone on the sofa, and with my feet rested on the tufted ottoman, I clicked on the TV. I was going to spend my night watching TV. 'How sad was I? This sad,' I laughed to myself, selecting *Dirty Dancing* from the TV screen. I couldn't help but laugh and muttered to myself, 'If you are going to wallow, might as well kick it old-school.'

As the opening scene of the movie started with the family heading to the mountain resort, I was comforted by the soundtrack that I'd listened to at least one hundred times throughout my life.

About the same time, a knock on the door startled me. I paused the movie to check my phone to see if anyone had texted that they were dropping by. It was highly unlikely that any of my staff would just show up at the door unannounced. They knew better than that.

The knock sounded again. It was aggressive, almost like a police knock. I wished that I was in my city house with its fancy peephole and video system, but the bunkie didn't have any of those things - just a screen door. There was no hiding.

It was Dylan. I was surprised to see him, but since he'd already seen me, I couldn't pretend to not be home. The screen door groaned as I opened it towards him.

"What are you doing here?" I asked.

The last of the sun's golden rays passing through the pine trees cast a golden glow around Dylan's dark brown shaggy hair. I wondered if he knew how good-looking he was, as his six-foot-four stature towered in the doorframe.

"I wanted to invite you to a pizza party."

"A pizza party?" "Will there be party hats and grab bags?" I laughed, trying to make a joke. It had to be a joke, right? Who gets invited to a pizza party in their 20s?

Dylan had a way of smiling that made my body heat up

from the inside. And he did it now as he stood in the doorway. He took the Laketown Otters' hat off of his head and put it on mine.

"I could stop and get another baseball hat if you want to wear a hat to the party."

I took the cap off my head and handed it to him. "No thanks, I have plans tonight."

Dylan glanced behind me, does that plan include a bowl of popcorn and the movie *Dirty Dancing?*"

I looked behind me and could clearly see Jennifer Grey's face paused midsentence on the screen and heaping bowl of popcorn on the table. "It's not your business what my plans are tonight. The only thing you need to know is that they don't include you." I don't know where the attitude came from, and I immediately regretted it.

Dylan stood straight in the doorway and smoothed his T-shirt out before crossing his arms across his well-defined chest. His eyes looked a little sad and he glanced on the ground before meeting my gaze. "I guess you don't want your boat done then, do you?"

"Hey, we already have a deal for the boat. You can't change the terms now."

"I guess that's true." The softness had returned to his eyes. "Kane and Jessie are having people over to Pine Hill for pizza and hockey on a big screen." His eyes crinkled as he smiled, "And for some reason, I thought that you might be interested in going."

It was utterly ridiculous – and completely sweet. "Me?" I pointed to my chest. "Do you see a bunch of empty beer cans and a pink camouflage hat somewhere?" I joked and hoped that he found it funny. I was basically throwing out the only stereotype I know about Laketownie girls. They could crush beers like the guys and usually had some form of camo print on their bodies at all times.

Dylan laughed and rubbed the back of his neck. "You know Kane and Jessie. I thought you might want to get out of this castle."

"Are you asking me on a date?" My heart had sped up and I hoped that Dylan didn't notice the shakiness in my voice. "You know that we aren't dating material."

His lips pursed like I had hurt his feelings. "No. We're going to tell everyone that we're friends."

It had been hot, having a guy in Laketown with no strings attached. At least, I felt that way and I'm pretty sure that he did too. During the entire time we had been together we never talked about getting serious. I thought it was an unspoken agreement. I never told him that I didn't sleep with anyone else but him.

"Is that true?" I asked. "Technically, you're blackmailing me into hanging out with you. I think that there might be another word for that."

The mischievous glint returned to his eyes. "Friends with benefits."

"In your dreams, Moss. Those days are over. Now, I think we're…" I tapped my chin trying to think of something witty, but his damn eyelashes had rendered my brain useless.

"Ex-friends with benefits."

I couldn't help the smile. "Alright, come on. Let's go." I smacked his hard abs and then turned off the TV.

"You're coming?" His eyebrows shot up.

"Sure. As long as we tell everyone we're just friends. It might make the wedding date story thing a little more believable."

He nodded. "Good point."

The two of us headed to the driveway – a good five-minute walk from the bunkie where I stopped dead in my tracks. "What's that?" I pointed to the motorcycle parked in front of the carriage house.

"It's a dirt bike – a classic KTM." He beamed.

"It's a motorcycle." I was unimpressed with whatever kind of motorcycle he had just cited. I hadn't read any baby books yet, but I'm pretty sure getting on the back of a motorcycle in a silk dress with your unsuspecting baby daddy wasn't on the list of acceptable three-month pregnancy recommendations. "I can't get on that."

"Sure you can." He jogged to the motorcycle and pulled a black helmet from one of the leather bags on the side. "I brought you a helmet."

I crossed my arms. The flags above the garage doors flapped as the breeze picked up. "Dylan Moss. I'm not getting on the back of that motorcycle."

"Why? I'll take it easy. I promise." He held his hand up with his index and middle finger extended.

"What's that? A gang signal?" I wrapped my fingers around the weird gesture he'd made with his fingers.

Dylan laughed so hard I could see his stomach moving beneath his white T-shirt. "Kind of. It's the Boy Scouts' honor. I thought everyone knew it."

I shrugged. I had wanted to go to camp as a kid, a real camp where you learned to make fires and shelters, but instead, my parents had sent me to tennis and riding camps in Europe, where they didn't teach the Boy Scouts of America hand signals.

"It doesn't matter if you don't start it and push that bike with your feet. I'm not getting on that back of it." I pointed to the orange bike.

"Well, Princess? How are we going to get to the ball?" He put the helmet away and leaned on his bike. A real modern-day James Dean was two feet from me, and I could feel my palms start to sweat as he stared me down. When I met Dylan, I thought he was hot, but I swear, every time I saw the man, he got even better looking. His wavy hair, chiseled jawline, and perfect biceps, combined with that bike were a recipe for panty removal.

"Does this make you Prince un-Charming?" I laughed.

He was fighting a smile; I could see it. "Since we're all about deals, I'll make you one. I'll go to this pizza party with you, but not on that death machine." I swirled my finger as I pointed to the bike. "I'll let you pick any car from the carriage house or boat from the boathouse."

He stood and smoothed his T-shirt just as a drop of rain fell from the sky. We both looked up and the dark clouds from earlier had collected over the Yates' estate. "I vote for something from the carriage house." He grabbed my hand, and we ran to the building where I punched in the code for the garage. Inside, the fluorescent lights flickered and then my family's northern car collection came into view.

Dylan whistled. "Any car?"

I glanced at the collection, but my word was my word. "Any."

He sucked in his breath and meandered through the space between the parked cars, dragging his fingertip along hoods and over door handles. "Even this one?" He pointed to a classic red Ferrari.

"Even that one," I smiled. He looked like a kid in a candy store. "But it looks best as a convertible, and I'm pretty sure we're going to get wet tonight." I knew it was a double entendre but didn't let on that it was intentional. There was no way to describe the way Dylan moved, other than like a real man. His broad shoulders were squared, and he had a carefree swagger that oozed confidence.

"It's a tough call." He yelled from the far side of the garage. "This dually is super nice, but so is this Rolls Royce."

"Dually?" My footsteps echoed on the polished concrete as I joined Dylan.

"The pickup." He pointed to the big work truck that was parked outside the garage.

"Done." I laughed and skipped to the safe that held the keys and returned with the gold RR keys and tossed them to him.

"Really?" He stared at the keys in his hand.

"You don't expect a princess to show up to a party in a… dually, do you?"

"But of course not." He jogged to the passenger side of the silver Rolls Royce and opened up one of the suicide doors for me. "Your chariot awaits."

I slid into the classic car and when Dylan started it up, I felt the power of the engine throughout my entire body. I wasn't sure if it was the power of the engine or the feeling of being in the car with Dylan that had my body prickling.

Dylan drove the car a lot more respectfully than I thought he would, and on the way to Pine Hill, I found myself admiring his toned arms and the way his thigh muscles filled out his jeans. I didn't know whether it was the pregnancy hormones or the feeling of guilt for not telling Dylan about the baby, nor planning to – ever, that had tears welling up in my eyes.

Luckily the sun had set and I was pretty sure that in the twilight, the extra shimmer in my eyes wouldn't be noticeable. Especially when Dylan turned onto Mustang Point Road and his eyes were trained on the curvy trail that led to Kane Fitzgerald's family cottage.

"Do you know if your sister has her dress yet?" It was small talk, but I felt like I had to say something. I blinked hard, stopping the tears from actually falling, but kept staring out the window at shadows in the forest.

"You'll have to ask her. She told me they were getting married and that I was going to walk her down the aisle. That's it."

"You're walking her down the aisle? That's so sweet." I turned to look at his profile.

He nodded. "I wish my dad was there to do it, but…" he shrugged.

Dylan had talked about his mom and dad a few times, and I knew that he had struggled without them. I slipped my hand over his and he spread his fingers so I could interlace mine with his. "You're going to do an amazing job giving your sister away. It will be a nice thing to see." It was the first time I'd thought positively about attending the wedding. Right after he asked me, all I'd done was worry about the paparazzi and how I would explain the very prominent baby bump. I had forgotten about dancing the night away to a cheesy wedding band, laughing at speeches, and trying hard to pretend I didn't want to catch the bouquet.

As we pulled to a stop in front of Pine Hill, I pulled my hand away from his, but he snatched it and kissed the back of it.

"Thank you," he said.

"For what?" He was still holding onto my hand.

"For being my friend." His eyes met mine and all I wanted to do was kiss him, even though it felt like we had just drawn a new line in the sand of our relationship. We were friends without benefits. But we were friends. A friendship with Dylan felt more real than any of the other friends I'd made in Laketown. As much as I wanted to reach my hands around his thick neck and feel his lips on mine one more time, I knew that we'd entered a new phase in our relationship.

"You're welcome, Moss."

He grinned. "Moss?"

I smiled coyly at him. "Isn't that what friends do? Call each other by their last name?"

He kissed my hand again, then set it on my leg and patted it. "If you say so, Yates."

We both laughed and Dylan stepped out of the car and ran to open the passenger door for me.

We had driven out of the rain from the Yates Estate, but the wind had a warmth to it and as we walked to the entranceway of Pine Hill, side-by-side, a few questions were swirling around in my head.

The biggest of which was, why couldn't my parents approve of a man like Dylan? Sure, he was a little rough around the edges, but as the moon peeked out from behind the clouds and lit the way down the flagstone pathway, Dylan's skin glowed in its light, and he looked fucking perfect.

TEN
DYLAN

IN LAKETOWN, the wind usually blows cold. Growing up, my dad used to say that when the wind blew from the north in the summer, that storms were coming. Tonight, the wind was coming straight from the south and if I closed my eyes, it felt like Bronwyn and her pretty yellow dress were swirling around in the warm Caribbean breeze.

Jessie met us at the door of her fiancé's cottage. Kane's dad was a bigwig financier, who as far as I knew, spent his entire life working and rarely spent any time up at the cottage so Kane had the place to himself. And now, so did my little sister. She looked right at home opening up that big oak door, the laughter from behind her, warm and inviting.

"Come on in."

I stepped aside and gestured for Bronwyn to go ahead of me.

"Bronwyn," Jessie opened up her arms and to my surprise, Bronwyn hugged her. Jesse had said that she knew Bronwyn, but I didn't think that they were on hugging terms.

"Nice to see you, Jessie." Bronwyn and I followed Jessie

into the kitchen. Jessie opened the fridge, asking, "What can I get you?"

Bronwyn and I both spoke at the same time, 'seltzer'. We looked at each other and laughed. Jesse smiled at us and cracked open a bottle of sparkling water.

"Have you got any lemon?" Bronwyn asked

"You bet," Jesse smiled and handed the glasses of sparkling water to us. She elbowed Bronwyn and whispered, "There's a keg down at the big screen."

"Thanks," Bronwyn said. I didn't see her as much of a beer drinker, she was more of the champagne type.

"Have you got any bubbly?" I asked.

"I think so. I can go check," Jesse said. Bronwyn grabbed her by the arm.

"No, no, no. It's okay. I'm on a cleanse at the moment."

"I get it," Jesse smiled. "When I'm in training, I don't drink anything but water and maybe some electrolytes." Jesse put her hand on my lower back and Bronwyn's as well. "Come on. Everyone is down at the boat house."

It was the perfect night. Jesse and Kane had set up a huge screen on the top of the boat house and they were playing classic hockey movies. Kane's chef stood in front of an authentic Italian homemade pizza oven and took orders for everyone's individual pie. I expected Bronwyn to get something either vegetarian, or boring, but she surprised me and got a Margherita pizza. I opted for the meat lovers.

One thing I noticed about this party, was that it was all couples, and I was glad that I'd stopped to get Bronwyn. Brody Bishop and his girlfriend, Brianna, who I hadn't seen for years, were there, as well as Leo and his girlfriend, Faith. One of Kane's National League friends, a guy named Wayne, was there with a pretty wife named, Bianca.

"You're Bronwyn Yates," Bianca got up from her chair to give Bronwyn not one, but two kisses on the cheek. I had seen people greet with kisses in the movies, but never in real life. It was kind of hot and my jeans felt a little tighter in the crotch region. *She's just your friend*, I whispered to myself, and took a sip of my water. Beer had always given me a little extra courage with the ladies, but with Brownyn, it was different. She riffed with me in a way that felt so natural. I glanced at her, now in full conversation with all the ladies at the party, the perfect angles of her face highlighted by the twinkle lights strung over the deck of the boathouse.

Kane sat in the chair next to mine. "Look at that hen party over there," he gestured with his beer glass. "They didn't even see that classic Domi hit."

"It was a good one." I laughed. "Almost as good as the one Leo gave to Lockwood the last time we played the Bobcats." Leo, the assistant coach had been a player – and had a rivalry with Gunnar Lockwood, one of the top players in the league. And both of them had been into Faith.

Kane tossed some sunflower seeds into his mouth and then handed me the bag. "I heard about that. Leveled that cocky s.o.b."

I took a handful of sunflower seeds and was about to put them all in my mouth at once when my eyes met Bronwyn's. Just like in the movies, everything disappeared around me and it felt like we were the only two people in the world at that moment. When she smiled and looked away, the momentary spell was broken. Knowing that it would happen again, there was no way I'd be able to not look at her for the rest of the night. I bit the shell of one sunflower seed at a time and tried not to look.

THE PIZZAS WERE SERVED, and we all came together at the long table in the center of the boathouse. Candles flickered and each place setting was complete with heavy silverware and real napkins. Bronwyn slid into her seat beside me, and the unexpected touch of her hand on my shoulder caught me off guard and I twitched.

"A little jumpy?" She draped the napkin across her lap.

I followed suit, wondering if she would eat her pizza with a knife and fork.

"Are you having a good time?" I whispered as everyone got settled.

Her smile was broad and wide. "I am."

Jessie sat on the other side of me. "Dyl. Did you know that Bronwyn and Kane went on a date years ago?"

"It wasn't a date," Bronwyn and Kane said at the same time.

I kind of remembered a little bit of drama, but that was before Bronwyn and I first hooked up.

"Really?" I raised my eyebrows at her.

"Kane's stepmom—"

"Ex-stepmom." Kane interrupted.

Bronwyn nodded. Her eyes sparkled in the candlelight. "I thought it was a date. Kane's former stepmom, one of the worst human beings I've ever met, by the way..." her eyes shot to Kane and he nodded in agreement, "She told me it was a date, but as soon as I saw the way he looked at your sister, I knew I didn't have a shot."

I twitched again, but this time it was in response to Bronwyn's hand on my thigh. "That night turned out way better anyway."

The beer had been flowing heavily that night, but not so much that I forgot meeting the most beautiful woman in Laketown – Brownyn Yates. "I didn't know you were on a date with Kane that night," I said.

"It wasn't a date," Kane repeated.

"And look how it worked out." She raised her glass. "To Jessie and Kane."

The individual conversations paused, and everyone raised their glasses. The lake lapping against the rocky shoreline was briefly quieted by the tinkling of glasses as we all toasted to the bride and groom.

The pizzas were incredible and when Bronwyn folded her piece in half and picked it to take a giant bite, it was one of the sexiest things I'd ever seen.

Kane made sure the drinks were topped up and when we were all stuffed, he turned to Bronwyn and me. "That evening brought me and Jessie together, but it looks like we're not the only couple that found each other that night." His eyes were a little glassy, and his words, while sweet and slightly uncharacteristic, were slurred.

"We're not a couple," Bronwyn and I said at the same time.

"Could've fooled me," Kane laughed. He stood and made his way to the keg. I glanced around and for the first time that night, nobody was looking at us. Jessie and Kane were helping the staff clear the dishes and the other couples were leaning over the railing, pointing at something across the lake.

If I were drunk, I would've blamed the booze, but I was one hundred percent sober, and while everyone was preoccupied, I turned to Bronwyn and pulled the napkin from her lap with my left hand and replaced it with my right hand, feeling the tautness of her thigh under the silky fabric. After another glance confirmed everyone was still occupied, I kissed her. Not hard and angry like on the dock, but soft and sweet, like she had been all night. I felt her thigh tense under my hand and her body melt towards mine for a brief moment.

Too brief.

The vibration of the deck boards told me that someone was in motion. We jerked apart from each other, but I squeezed her thigh before letting go.

She stood. "I have to go to the ladies' room."

Jessie took her place. "I saw that," she whispered to me. "You two aren't fooling anybody."

"We're just friends, Jess."

"Says who?" she leaned her elbow on the table.

"We agreed on it. It was, you know, a mutual thing." The more I thought about it, the more I wanted to be with her. I didn't want to be Bronwyn's friend and I sure as hell didn't want to be her fuckboy anymore either.

"We're from two separate worlds."

"Did she say that?" There was a hint of hardness in my sister's voice.

"No, she's never said anything like that."

Jessie softened. "Dylan. Look at me and Kane. Don't sell yourself short. She saw the way Kane looked at me years ago, and I see the way you two are looking at each other tonight. Don't be stupid. Life's too short."

We weren't overly affectionate siblings, but Jessie gave me a hug before she left.

For a moment I was alone at the table, underneath the cloudy Laketown sky with Jessie's words skating around in my head. I had always just assumed that Bronwyn would be with some rich dude who could provide her with yachts and expensive clothes. She would never actually want to be with a small-town mechanic like me, would she?

A flicker of yellow caught my eye as Bronwyn's dress flapped like a flag in the breeze. I knew that the clouds had parted without looking to the sky by the way her white-blond hair glowed.

Jessie was right. Life was short and I had never felt a connection to any person like I had with Bronwyn. I knew when she was looking at me, I could feel it. I knew when she was close. I could feel her without touching her.

"Want to take a walk?" I asked.

"A walk?"

My stomach felt jittery all of sudden like I'd just skated my heart out and was about to barf. "Yeah, there's something I want to talk to you about."

She paused as if she were thinking about it and the thudding of my heart ceased echoing in my ears.

"Okay." Her voice was quiet, and she pulled me from my seat at the table and just like that, my heartbeat was back, thudding louder than ever.

ELEVEN
BRONWYN

MY HEELS TAPPED along Pine Hill's walkway. The limestone path was lined with small iron lights that lit up the ground enough to see where we were going, but not too much to ruin the cloak of darkness between Dylan and me.

My dress swirled around my ankles, and I felt it catch on one of the heels. I stumbled, but Dylan caught my elbow.

"I think I'm going to take these off." I stopped and balanced on one leg while I tried to undo the shoe.

Dylan held my elbow, but with only one hand free, I struggled with the tiny buckle. "Let me," he offered and dropped to his knee. "Hold onto my shoulder."

I let my fingers rest on him, feeling the muscles beneath his T-shirt and their subtle movements as he undid each of my shoes.

"Thank you." I accepted the shoes, and my feet practically breathed a sigh of relief as they were released from the confines of the leather. "They're not the most practical."

"But they look good," he laughed.

"They do."

We walked a few more steps in silence, the sound of the

waves getting softer the farther we got from the lake along with those of the drunken card game we'd left behind at the boathouse disappearing. "It's a beautiful night." It was really just an okay night. It was like Mother Nature didn't know what to do with the evening, she threatened sprinkles one minute and then provided clear bright skies the next.

"It is a beautiful night." Through my peripheral vision, I could see Dylan looking at me. I was so torn. I wanted to disappear into the night with him, to feel his hands over every inch of my body – but on the other hand, I couldn't see a way to make it work. I felt like a boat in the center of a hurricane, everywhere I looked – there was a mess. I couldn't fool around with Dylan or his heart and keep the secret in my belly from him. Being with him meant giving up my inheritance, and it sounds shallow, but what would happen if I gave it all up – and he didn't want to be with me anyway?

We walked further away from the main cottage, the path winding past smaller outbuildings. "You're awfully quiet," he said.

I couldn't tell him what was going on inside my head. "I'm just enjoying the evening," I lied.

Well, only somewhat. I was enjoying the evening with him. It had been one of the best in my entire life. His friends were real people who didn't care about my last name, or that I came from the Yates Estate. I drank beer, ate pizza, laughed, and felt my heart race every time my eyes met Dylan's.

"Bron." His voice sounded serious. He stopped walking.

"Yes?" I turned so our bodies were facing each other, but his face was in shadow.

"You and me." He stared up at the sky. "We've known each other for years."

Known. That was an interesting way of putting it.

"We have." I didn't know what else to say.

"Why have we never talked about being together?"

He was thinking the same thing I was. "I guess it never came up. And then you went through that rough patch. When we reconnected this spring, I thought you just wanted to have some fun."

"That's what I thought you wanted."

I smiled but didn't know if he could see it. "I did have fun." I don't know why, but my throat constricted, and I felt like I was going to cry.

"Me too."

He reached out to hold my hands. "Being around you, I don't know how to describe it, it just feels right." He rubbed the back of my hands with his thumbs. For someone who worked with his hands, they were surprisingly soft.

I knew that I shouldn't ask, but I couldn't stop myself. "What are you getting at? What do you want?" My voice was a little colder than I wanted it to be.

He let go of my hands and ran one of his through his hair. "Isn't it obvious, Bron?

I studied the pathway at my feet. It was totally obvious. "No, Dylan. What do you want?" My parents' many lectures about men without money using me for mine were nagging at the back of my brain.

"You. Bron. I want you. I always have, always will." His voice had dropped almost an octave and into growl territory.

The wind whipped my dress against my legs and this time there was a chill in its gust.

"Say something." He took a step closer.

Oh, God. I could smell him. A desire for his touch coursed through my body. I knew what his dick felt like and there was nothing I wanted more than to feel his girth pushing into me. I took a step back; my body was going to betray me, and I needed to think straight.

He stepped closer and into the light. His eyes were filled with intensity and were smoldering as they searched mine.

All I wanted to do was launch myself into his arms. "Tell me you don't want to be with me." He closed the gap between us, and I could feel the heat of his body on my collarbone. "And give me one good reason we can't be together."

There was one very good reason we couldn't be together. BUT it was the same good reason why we SHOULD be together. At that moment, I hated being a Yates. I hated being the heiress to a billion-dollar fortune and the rules that had been imposed on my life.

I opened my mouth, hoping that something good would come out of it. Instead, I stood in front of the man I was falling in love with, trying to figure out what the hell to tell him.

"Time's up," he growled. Dylan grabbed my hips and pulled them to his. A gasp escaped from my open mouth, but only briefly before Dylan's lips were on mine. I didn't resist, I melted into his roughness, my body needing this assertive man. My hands found the back of his strong neck and I returned the kiss, pressing myself against him, not worrying if he noticed that my body had changed since the last time he'd touched it.

The flags on the building behind us snapped angrily and the hem of my dress whipped against my legs. My skin prickled with goosebumps as the breeze escalated into a gale, but I didn't notice. I was too wrapped up in the warmth of Dylan's embrace, the softness of his lips, and the very big, very hard bulge at the front of his jeans pressing against me.

I was more turned on than I'd ever been in my entire life.

The first drops of rain fell like marbles around us, bouncing off the hard stones, but it didn't stop either of our hands from exploring each other's bodies while we kissed. Mine went to his T-shirt and rested on his lower abs and the sexy muscles that disappeared into the waistband of his jeans. One of his hands rested on my shoulder, while the other held a fist full of my dress and my ass at the same time.

The next drops landed on us, almost hard enough to hurt. But I didn't care. Dylan's other hand found its way to my ass and he pulled me to him tightly. I longed to get closer to him. I wrapped my leg around him and pressed my body so hard against his that I couldn't tell where mine stopped and his started. My breaths were coming hard and fast and my hands gripped either side of Dylan's face, my lips wanting more. A rumble of thunder sounded in the distance, and while I heard it somewhere in my subconscious, I ignored it. Dylan squeezed my ass and then dropped my dress from his hands, falling softly around my calves. There was one more crack of thunder and the sky light lit up with lightning, not the jagged showstopper lightning, the stretch across the whole sky kind of lightning. I looked into Dylan's eyes as the light flashed around us and felt like I could see his soul. It scared me a little bit, I'd never seen anyone that intensely before.

Dylan kissed me once more then whispered, "I should get you out of the rain."

The drops turned to streams that turned to sheets and within seconds it was like someone had just turned on a tap.

"Come on." Dylan grabbed my hand and I squealed as he pulled me along the pathway.

"I thought that the trees would shelter us, but they're not doing a very good job." He laughed as the rain streaming down his face dripped off the end of his nose and beaded on his eyelashes.

"I wonder if any of these cabins are open?" Dylan looked past me at one of the small guest bunkies.

"We shouldn't," I said. But secretly, the idea of sneaking into one of Pine Hill's bunkies with Dylan Moss was so rebellious and scandalous, it was something I absolutely needed to do.

"I know we shouldn't," he smiled. "But we are going to." Holding my hand, we ran to the screen door of the green building. Dylan tried the door, shaking the knob comically, but the cabin was locked up tight.

With the chill of the weather, the goosebumps I had from kissing Dylan had turned into goosebumps from being cold. My lips started to chatter. "We should go back to the main house," I suggested.

"We should," Dylan said. Lightning flashed and I saw the small-town rebel that had caught my eye so many years ago. "But we're not going to do that." He scooped me up into his arms and I buried my face into his neck as he carried me along the pathway, wondering where we were going. When I realized he was taking me to the car my heart dropped with disappointment. Was he taking me home?

He opened the door to the Rolls-Royce but instead of helping me into the front seat, he crawled into the back seat and pulled me in behind him. This was even better than the Pine Hill cabin - kissing my small-town mechanic boyfriend in the back of my family's Rolls-Royce seemed like the ultimate act of defiance. All of the anger I felt at my family for forcing these decisions on me made me want to defile the backseat of that car with Dylan, in every way possible.

"We don't want to wreck the interior," Dylan whispered. He pulled his wet T-shirt over his head and I heard it thud heavily onto the floor. "Let's get you out of that dress."

I gave him my best smoldering look and maneuvered so that I was face down on the rear seat, exposing the zipper on the back of my dress to him. My body tensed as I felt his legs straddle either side of me. He held onto the bodice of my dress and slowly, one tang at a time, unzipped my dress. By the time he slipped the straps off my shoulders and slid the dress off my body, every inch of me was buzzing with anticipation and I turned over beneath him, to look him in the eyes.

"You're so beautiful," he whispered. He traced my body with his fingertips, starting at my collarbone, lightly following the lace of my bra, and pausing to draw circles around my nipples with his thumbs. He kissed my chest between my breasts while his hands slipped behind me to unhook my bra. When I felt the warmth of his palms on my nipples a moan escaped through my lips.

"Oh, Dylan," I whispered into his mouth. "I've missed you so damn much."

"Did you miss me? Or my dick?" His mouth was still on mine. It could've sounded crass, but it was one of the hottest things he'd ever said to me.

"They're a package deal aren't they?" I reached my hand to the front of his soaking wet jeans and had to use two hands to get the top button undone. The zipper followed easily, and I thrust my hands into the back of his jeans and started to pull them down. When I couldn't reach any further, I brought my feet up to hook onto the belt loops and pulled his wet jeans down to his ankles. I gasped as his cock slapped against me with a loud thud. It shouldn't have been such a surprise to me, Dylan never wore underwear.

"Still rocking the commando?"

"You know it." His breath was hot on my ear. Dylan held both of my wrists in one of his hands and cupped my cheek with the other while he kissed me again. I writhed beneath him, pushing myself closer to his body urging him to lower down onto me so I could feel his weight. I just wanted to be covered in Dylan.

"I've missed you, Dylan."

He stopped kissing me and stared into my eyes. I repeated it. "I've missed you." I rested my hand on his chest.

"I've missed you too, Bronwyn."

"Missed me? Or missed fucking me?"

His brow furrowed and all the muscles tightened in his body. "Bronwyn, before we got soaking wet, I told you that all I wanted was you." He tapped my chest and I could feel the power in his finger on my sternum. He tapped it again. "You," he whispered and then rested his hand over my heart.

All of a sudden, it felt wrong. "I can't do this."

"What can't you do?" Dylan asked. He brushed my wet hair behind my ear and stared at me, his blue eyes searching mine.

What could I tell him? All of a sudden, I went from being super horny to realizing that I could not have sex with the man. There was no way, no matter how horny I got, that I could have sex with him and not feel guilty about it.

"Dylan?"

"Yes?" He eased his body off of mine and sat upright. I pulled my legs off of his and sat so I could face him, my bra straps hanging loosely off my shoulders.

"Here, let me get that." He reached around me, and I could feel his breath on my neck as he clipped up the bra.

"I have a weird question for you."

"Okay…"

"If we were to meet now, do you think we could or would, you know, go on dates?"

He chuckled. "You want to go on dates? With me? In Laketown?"

"It was just a hypothetical question."

Dylan crossed arms and looked like he was thinking. "Well…" He let out a small laugh. "If, hypothetically, you and I want to go on some dates. I would probably take you to the fall fair. It's a big deal in Laketown."

All of the best romance movies I'd ever seen started to flash before my eyes – mostly kissing on Ferris wheels. "I've never been to a small-town fair. Would you win me a big stuffed animal?"

He rubbed his hands on his thighs. He was sitting completely naked with a semi-hard-on in the back of the Rolls-Royce. But… he didn't seem to care.

"I'd win you a stuffed animal so big you wouldn't be able to carry it." He shifted closer to me and draped his arm over my shoulders. "For the next date, I'd take you fishing."

"I've been fishing," I said.

"Not this kind of fishing," he laughed. "I'd make you paddle the canoe."

I laughed and smacked his thigh. The idea seemed so ridiculous. "You've got to be joking." I rested my head on his chest and let my hand rest on his thighs.

"It's no joke, Bron."

I could feel his heart beating and the baritone of his voice against my cheek made me smile. "Tell me more," I purred, caressing a little higher on his thighs.

He absentmindedly played with the end of my hair, and I wondered what he was thinking. The vibration from his voice on my cheek and the sound of the rain hitting the top of the car were the only things I could hear. "I would call your friends and find out what you wanted to do, and we would do that."

I gave him another little slap. "That's cheating," I teased. "I want to hear what you would come up with."

This time, my fingertips brushed the base of his shaft and his cock twitched in response. His heartbeat quickened, thudding under my cheekbone. "I'd make you watch one of my hockey games." His chest shook a little as he chuckled.

I moved from my blissful position on his chest so I could look him in the face, "I'd love to see you play hockey."

"You would?"

"You seem surprised." I had moved my caressing from his thighs to lightly gripping his now fully rock-hard cock.

"Yeah, I've heard so much about the star of the Otters."

"I'm not the star."

"That's not what I've heard." I gripped onto his manhood a little tighter and he arched his hips and shifted in the seat. I swung my leg over his, so I was straddling him and held onto his shoulder with my free hand while my other hand continued to caress him. His eyes were hooded but yet still intently staring at me. "I've heard that you're one of the most underrated players."

A line of crimson spread across his jawbone.

"Dylan Moss. Are you blushing?"

He wrapped his hand around mine which was wrapped around his manhood and grinned slyly. "I mean, you do have your hands on my cock."

It was clear that he was brushing off the compliment. I kissed along his jawbone and then let my lips linger on his until we both batted our eyes open at the same time. "Dylan, do you think you could take me on a date, for real?"

"Yeah, babe." He squeezed my ass.

It didn't make sense, but my heart took over the operation of my words and totally turned off my brain. At that moment, all rational thinking had been thrown out the window. "I want to start over with you. I want to pretend like we've just met and haven't been hooking up for the past two years."

"That sounds like fun." His strong hands were going to leave fingermarks in my ass, and I loved it.

"The only thing." I paused the stroking, and he opened his eyes a little wider. I kissed him again. "Do you think we can keep it a secret – for now?"

His lips narrowed and I knew I'd upset him. His hands

slipped from my butt, but he kept them looped around me. "You want to go on dates with me. And keep it a secret."

I nodded.

"You're going to have to tell me why."

I hadn't gotten this far in my spontaneous plan. I knew that I wanted to be around Dylan, and my body wanted to make love to him with an intensity that I couldn't explain – but until I figured out how, and if I was going to tell him about the baby, I couldn't have sex with him. I realized that it was selfish of me, to keep him in my life on my terms – new terms.

I picked at my thumbnail while I tried to think of how to explain it in a way that would make sense.

"Are you embarrassed to be seen with me?" His voice was low, not embarrassed, but accusatory and I felt his body tense beneath me.

"No!" I couldn't have said it more emphatically and repeated it again softly. "Not at all."

He relaxed. "Then, why, Bron? This seems a little…"

"Weird," we said it together and I couldn't help but smile.

"I know." I let the words come out. "But, the paparazzi, they're going to be all over this story. There's some stuff happening overseas with Yates Petroleum and my family wants to stay out of the limelight. And…" I rested my hand on his chest. "I don't want them to go after you. They'll dig into your background. I'm used to it, but I wouldn't wish that kind of scrutiny on anyone. Dylan, they'll write about your parents."

He nodded slowly and I could see the words sinking in.

"And my parents, they don't know about the struggles you've had and until they get to know you, I don't want that kind of publicity for us."

It was all true. To some extent. The photographers would hound us. Pictures of the car wreck where his parents died would turn up in the gossip magazines. If they decided to be cruel, his struggle with alcohol and whatever else would be made public. Was it still a lie if I just left out a few things?

The car was so steamy that drops of condensation streamed down the windows, but the rainfall had slowed. Dylan kissed one of my breasts. "So, this. We have to pretend like this…" he bit at the nipple, "…has never happened?"

"Well, maybe we don't have to go back to the very beginning," I kissed his neck and then shifted my knees to the floor of the car and continued kissing down his chest.

My plan didn't make any sense. Maybe it was the pregnancy hormones turning me into a sex fiend. Whatever it was, I took Dylan's manhood into my mouth and studied his face as I worked his shaft. I knew the way he liked it and it wasn't long before his hips bucked, and he moaned as his body shuddered with his orgasm.

As I rested my head on his strong hockey player thighs, thoughts raced through my mind. What had I just done? I didn't see a way out of this. It was as though I had become addicted to Dylan and couldn't get him out of my life. But there was no way this could end well. Without a doubt, I was going to get hurt, I knew that. What was this going to do to Dylan? I squeezed my eyes shut and justified everything. I was getting what I wanted, for now, and so was he.

TWELVE
DYLAN

Some people might find the smell of a marina, overheated engines, and engine oil, a little off-putting, but when I walked into work, it felt like home. My dad had been a mechanic, and in some way, the smell of the marina reminded me of him.

I should've felt like shit. I was wearing the same clothes I'd worn the night before – and they were still damp. I'd fallen asleep for maybe an hour – two tops, underneath a blanket of a yellow silk dress in the back of a Rolls Royce, which, if you have to sleep in the back of a car, a Rolls is the way to go. I was on my third coffee. Floyd bought one of those expensive cappuccino makers to make coffee for all the rich people while they waited for their boats, and I was jittery. I don't think it was the coffee though. Adrenaline and excitement had coursed through my body since the conversation with Bronwyn, who technically, I think, was now my girlfriend – and who gave me the best blowjob I'd ever had in my life.

As I sanded my boat project, I tried to figure out when and where I could take her. With the announcement of the

National League Playoff Series, our practice schedule had doubled – and I needed to get the boat finished.

Before the marina officially opened was my favorite time of the day. I had the space to myself and could listen to whatever music, or podcasts that I wanted to – as loud as I wanted.

Today I had The Eagles, one of my dad's favorite bands, cranked loud enough to hear it over the sound of the sander and through my earplugs. As the chorus to *Hotel California* blared, I felt a firm hand grip my shoulder. My nerves were a jangled mess already and I must've jumped a foot in the air.

"Easy, kid," Floyd shouted.

I took one of my earplugs out and turned down the music. "I didn't hear you come in."

Floyd's shoulders shook as he laughed. "No shit." His eyes traveled past me to the frame of the boat. I had just started applying the cedar strips. "She's looking good."

"Thanks." I turned to look at my project. It had been a labor of love and proven to be easier than I thought.

"Long night, Moss?" There was concern in Floyd's eyes. Along with Coach Covington, Floyd had been one of the male father figures that had pulled me out of the downward spiral I had been riding a couple of years earlier.

I tried to stop the smile from spreading across my face. "Kind of, but the good kind."

My smile must've been contagious as one spread across Floyd's face too. His white mustache twitched as he winked at me. "I remember those days."

Floyd wasn't the type to ask questions, and I was thankful for that because I wouldn't be able to lie to him. How were Bronwyn and I ever going to keep this dating thing a secret?

Part of me loved the idea of keeping it clandestine, it made it pretty damn exciting, but the other part of me just wanted to be with her, and, truthfully, be seen with her.

Floyd rapped his knuckle on the boat. "Solid work, kid. I might have a buyer for it – if you want to sell her."

"Really?" I didn't have a plan for the boat, it was just something I'd always wanted to do. "I'm not sure if I want to sell it."

"Well, if you do, let me know. And Moss. Don't sell your work short – this boat could fetch a lot of money with the right collector."

The idea of making money from something that I found so satisfying, like playing hockey, almost seemed like a foreign concept. "Well, I don't really have a place to moor her…" I would have to buy a trailer and keep the boat in the garage at my house.

"You know there's always a few extra slips here." Floyd adjusted the Otters' cap on his head, a Christmas present from me, and then headed to his office. He paused with his hand on the doorknob. "But you could always make another one. That's some serious talent you've got there."

Could the day get any better? A hot girl waiting for me to take her out and now, a potential collector wanting MY boat build. I had a full day of work, hopefully finishing off the engine on *Calliope* and then practice. Somewhere in there, I had to come up with an idea for an amazing date with Bronwyn - but how do you impress a billionaire?

After I finished as much as I could get done on the boat project, I knocked on the door to Floyd's office. I remembered something that Bronwyn had asked the night before.

"Hey, Floyd." I stood in the open door. "I'm open to selling the boat."

"I thought you might say that." He flipped through an old-fashioned Rolodex on his desk. "I'm going to make some calls for you."

"I thought that you had a buyer?" Was Floyd trying to pull something weird?

He laughed and gave me a sly smile. "I do. But it's better to have more than one – someone else wanting it makes 'em want it even more."

"Ah. I see." There was a reason Floyd had done so well in business. He looked like a bumpkin but was savvy like a big city businessman.

"Leave it with me, kid. Just get *Calliope* fixed up good and proper."

"I should be able to wrap it up today before practice." I lingered at the door. Not wanting to ask the next question, but I had promised Bronwyn.

"Is there something else?" Floyd put on his glasses and took a sip of his coffee.

"Yeah, um. A friend of mine was wondering about that cream you and your wife use on your hands."

His eyes bulged as he tried not to spit out his coffee. He swallowed. "Are you serious?"

I knew that this wasn't going to go over well. Floyd was as manly a man as they get. Another dude asking him about his hand lotion was going to seem, well, weird.

"Miss Yates..." I thought that if I threw her name into the conversation, he might be a little more forthcoming with the information, "... noticed that even though you work hard, your hands are very soft. She wants to know what you use on them." God, I felt dumb. And it wasn't Floyd's hands she'd remarked about, it was mine, but I couldn't tell Floyd that.

He rubbed his hands together. "She noticed, did she? He smiled beneath his bushy mustache. There's some in the bathroom and kitchen here, you should try it out – it's Thelma's homemade cream. You'll have to get a cup of tea with her and ask her what her secret ingredient is.

I knew he was mocking me at that point, but the joke was on him. I'd been using his fancy hand cream for months now

– and after hours of sanding, days in engines, and nights in hockey gloves, my hands had never felt better. "I'll ask her."

"Ask her what?" A voice spoke from behind me.

"Speak of the devil." Floyd got up from his desk and kissed his wife on the cheek. "Dylan wants your secret ingredient for your hand salve."

Thelma wrapped her chubby arm around my back and squeezed me. "If I told you, I'd hafta kill you."

"It's not for me." I laughed. "It's for Bronwyn Yates."

Her eyes sparkled when she looked at me. "Really? Lucky you, Mr. Moss."

My face flushed hot, and I hoped it wasn't as red as it felt. "We're just friends and I'm fixing her boat."

"Sure. Sure you are." She winked. "Floyd fixed my boat once too."

I knew that I was like a son to the two of them, but this conversation was too much. "Gross."

Their laugh sounded the same. I guess that's what spending years with the love of your life does to you. You start to sound and look the same.

Thelma had disappeared but returned with a small mason jar filled with a white cream. "Here, you give this to your friend." She put the jar in my hand and winked.

"Thanks, Thelma."

She patted my hand. "And you tell her if she wants some more to come and see me. I don't give out my secret recipe to just anyone."

Floyd and Thelma were the kindest, most giving people I knew, and their marriage, while I'm sure it had its ups and downs, seemed like one of the most solid ones out there. Maybe they were just from a different era, like my parents. If they were still alive, they'd be just as in love as these two. I knew it.

❄

HOCKEY PRACTICE that evening was brutal. Three guys puked. This playoff series had lit a fire in the Otters that I'd never seen in my four years with the team.

"What's going on?" Leo fell into stride next to me as the players filed out of the dressing room.

I kept walking. "What do you mean?"

"Your mind, it's not in the game. It's somewhere else."

I didn't think it was that obvious, but I had spent most of the game wondering whether Bronwyn would be interested in going fishing with me. I was also trying to figure out just how secretive she wanted this relationship to be. If it really was to keep the paparazzi away and to stop my name from being dragged through the mud, it might be easier to get a few more people involved in the story – like Jessie and Kane. I could also get some advice from Kane on how to wine and dine a rich lady, and hopefully, get some guidance from Jessie on the girl stuff. Bronwyn wasn't just a puck bunny who would be satisfied with tagging along to some games. She was a real woman, and if I was being honest with myself, I didn't know what the hell to do with a real woman.

"Sorry, man." I hated to admit that I wasn't one hundred percent into the practice.

"Coach noticed too." There was concern in Leo's voice. "Is everything okay?"

I took a deep breath. How long did I have to be a good boy before everyone stopped worrying about me falling to pieces? "Totally fine. Some big stuff is happening at work." That was true, the boat thing was huge for me, but the bigger stuff that was happening, the falling in love thing. Even if I wanted to, I couldn't tell anyone about that.

The sun was setting over the rooftops of Laketown as we stepped into the warm summer air. Leo walked with me the entire way to my beat-up Volvo. I could tell there was something else he wanted to say, but Leo didn't, or couldn't get it out. I shut my equipment in the trunk and Leo followed me to the driver's side. "What's up, Lion?" I still used his old hockey nickname.

He leaned in the open window. "I'm not supposed to say anything to you."

I groaned and pushed the key into the ignition but didn't turn it, letting my hands fall into my lap. "What the hell, Leo? Okay, then. Don't tell me." The gears of the ancient electric windows groaned as I pushed the button to close the window.

"Stop." Leo rested his hand on the glass. "There's a couple of scouts asking about you."

"Me?" The window shuddered as I lowered it. "I thought they wouldn't touch me or my antics with a ten-foot stick."

Leo laughed. "I didn't think they would either. You're not exactly what we in the business call 'coachable.'" He used air quotes. "But you're fast and you're skilled and you haven't pulled any shit in a long time. The league has noticed."

I rested my elbow on the frame of the open window. "You're not fucking around with me, are you? 'Cuz that would be pretty damn cruel." There was no way the scouts were looking at me. I thought that I had completely ruined my chance as a career hockey player years ago. My mind started to go as quickly as I skated a power-play – fast.

Leo cleared his throat. "I can already see you overthinking it."

I crossed my arms across my chest like armor. "Am not."

"Coach didn't want you to change anything. He thought that if you knew, you might start to do things differently, or the pressure..."

"The pressure might send poor wild card Dylan over the edge." I finished the sentence.

"No!" Leo interrupted. "You just might play a little differently."

"So, why are you telling me this then?"

Leo leaned down so he could look me in the eyes, his hands gripping the door of the car. "You were off today. That's all. You can't be off in the exhibition series, so whatever is on your mind, get it off your mind. If you want a career playing hockey. Got it?"

He patted the car a little too hard and bits of rust fell to the ground at his feet.

"Got it." My heart was pumping almost as fast as it had been in the Rolls Royce with Bronwyn.

"Good." Leo grinned. "You can do it, Moss. If not for any reason other than to get rid of this shitbox of a car."

"Hey, easy on the Vulva." I laughed. Jessie and I each had nicknames for the car we'd shared for years – hers was Penny, a reflection of the mostly rust color that had taken over the old station wagon, mine was just an immature play on words.

As I drove away from the rink, different scenes played in my mind. The biggest: it would be a hell of a lot easier for Bronwyn to be with a National League Player than a Lake-townie mechanic. I had two reasons to go all in for this series. One: I loved hockey and it had been my dream ever since I was a kid to make it – and two: well, it would impress the hell out of a certain model who had been occupying my mind for the past two years.

THIRTEEN
BRONWYN

THE TEXT MESSAGES were coming non-stop. Tess was blowing up my phone and every time it chimed, I felt my heart leap into my throat, hoping to see Dylan's name on the screen. This time it was Tess again. I picked up the phone and called her if only to put a stop to the incessant texting.

She wanted to go to a party on one of the islands and had begged me to come with her. The guest list was impressive, to her, but I didn't care about the Laketown who's who anymore. She wouldn't take no for an answer and told me she was coming over to drag my lame, skinny ass to the party. I had to pull out the big guns, and by big guns, I mean an excuse she couldn't counter.

"I'm having stomach issues." Any normal person would be able to read between the lines.

"I'll bring some Midol."

"Not period issues. The other kind." Part of me wished I was curled up on the couch with massive period cramps. My life would be a hell of a lot easier if I were in physical agony at the moment.

"You can mix your vodka with Pepto Bismol. Bron. You're not missing out on this party. I need my wing woman."

"Tess," I shouted before she could hang up the phone. "I have…I can't leave the house. *I have emergency-level diarrhea.*"

"Oh." There was silence on the other end of the line.

"Yes. Stomach issues." I couldn't believe that she'd made me come out and state what should've been obvious. "A normal person would understand that I can't be more than five steps from my bathroom."

The line was quiet for a moment. "That's pretty embarrassing, Bronwyn."

Now I was speaking her language. God forbid I embarrass her by crapping my La Perlas while watching her friends do keg stands.

With Tess off my back, I set my phone on the coffee table and resumed the movie I'd paused the night before. Johnny Castle and Baby were grinding on each other in the staff house – one of the best scenes in the movie.

I thought my phone chimed, but when I looked at it, there was nothing. Why hadn't he texted? Was he having second thoughts about the secret dating? I had gone for a swim, read *Vogue* magazine cover to cover while tanning on the deck of the boathouse, and had gone for a walk. All while keeping a close eye on my phone. I felt like a basket case. I never worried about a man texting me.

They always messaged me.

I knew he worked until five because that's when the marina closed, so when 6:00 rolled around I started doing something I swore I'd never do. Text a man first. I had several messages typed out on my phone but deleted them all.

There was a list of men I could message and they'd be at the door in a heartbeat – but they weren't Dylan. Was this what playing hard to get was all about? It sucked. Every second that went by, made me want him to message me even more.

This was no good. I was losing it. I had to get out of the house and do something before…

The phone chimed and I tried not to look at it. I was cool, calm, and collected. It didn't matter if Dylan messaged me. After all, it had been less than twenty-four hours since he dropped me in my wrinkly yellow dress and the Rolls Royce off as dawn was breaking.

This was bad and so not like me. Was this what it was like to truly like someone? *Really* like someone. If it was, I wasn't sure that I enjoyed the feeling – this was way out of my comfort zone. I resisted the urge to snatch up my phone and read the text message. I was Bronwyn Yates, whoever it was, could wait. I kept the movie playing and slipped into one of my favorite summer dresses, a white cotton gown with a smocked top, one that looked like it could be a vintage night-gown or have been on the set of *Little House on the Prairie*. I pulled up the hem and ran my hands over my belly, it looked like bloat as if I'd had a bit too much champers and brie at lunch. That's when I saw it. I leaned a little closer and gasped. I flicked on the overhead light and stood as close as I could to the mirror. My eyes weren't playing tricks on me, if I'd had hope that I could rejuvenate my career, it disappeared in a poof of smoke, or rather in the pale white of a tiny stretch mark.

"Nooooo." I flicked off the light and collapsed onto the sofa. I needed to talk to someone, but I hadn't told any of my friends about the pregnancy – yet. I sighed deeply and took a sip of my sparkling water as I realized just how empty and vacuous all of my friendships had been this far in my life. Hell, I felt more comfortable confiding in my interior designers and housekeeper than I did my own 'friends.' I was sure that once Tess found out I was no longer going to be on the party circuit, our friendship would be put on ice – the same with all of my model friends.

I shut my eyes for what felt like a minute, making a baby is apparently quite exhausting, and when I woke up, the credits to the movie were rolling. My phone buzzed and there was a text from Tess along with a blurry photo of Jake McManus with his shirt off. I had to admit, for a retired hockey player, his body was still top-notch. That's when I noticed the message from Dylan. It must have been the one that came in just before I fell asleep.

Just seeing his name on my phone made my lips turn into a smile. I clicked on the message and as my eyes scanned it, I sat bolt upright. It read:

Get ready for our first date. I'm coming to pick you up at seven-thirty.

The time on my phone read 7:20.

"Shit." I threw off the blanket and bolted to my bedroom. I couldn't go for a date looking like I had just wandered in from milking the cows in a previous century. I read the text again, hoping for a hint of what we were doing. Did I put on a dress with heels or something sporty and cute? Fucking men. They had no idea what we went through when it came to getting ready for a date – let alone a surprise date.

I opted for some black leggings and a black cashmere sweater over a black T-shirt. My hair had been piled into a messy bun on the top of my head and I shook it out, put on some minimal makeup, and finished my look with my state- ment red lipstick. As a model, I knew how to put myself together at a moment's notice.

My text back simply read: see you soon. I added a smiley face. Nothing too cutesy, but not cold either. Then, I put on some music, picked up a magazine, and took a seat on my screened-in porch, waiting for the sound of his sexy as hell- looking motorcycle to come down the driveway.

At 7:35, I still hadn't heard the motorcycle, so when Dylan appeared on my front stairs, I almost let out a scream.

"Hi." He smiled. "Did I scare you?"

Yes.

"No, I just didn't hear you drive in." I stood and opened the door to the porch. "Come in."

Dylan paused in the open door and produced a bouquet of flowers from behind his back. "These are for you."

It was the most beautiful bouquet I'd ever seen. The flowers were all different shades of pink. "They're beautiful." I put the bunch of flowers to my nose. "Let me put these in some water."

Before I could turn to head into the bunkie, Dylan's hand was on my wrist, and he was pulling me toward him. He snatched the flowers from my hand and tossed them into the woods.

"What are you doing—"

The second his lips were on mine I completely forgot about the flowers or anything else in the world besides Dylan. My knees wobbled and he pulled me a little tighter to him.

"My yard is full of those flowers. I'll get you more tomorrow." He whispered in my ear. "And then the next day… If you want them," he added.

I nodded and let my head rest on his chin. "I do want them." I kissed his lips again and then we locked eyes. "I want them every day."

"You got it, Queen," he growled.

I smiled. "Last time it was Princess, Did I get a promotion?"

"Nah." He squeezed both of my ass cheeks at the same time. "I was an idiot and didn't realize the power of the woman standing in front of me. You're no princess, B. You're a queen. All day, every day."

The whoosh of adrenaline that surged through my body following his words caught me off guard and I felt a little light-headed. I held onto his shoulders and hoped that I wouldn't fall. "And what does that make you?" I knew that he wouldn't say, Prince Charming, Dylan Moss was a lot of things, but predictable and cheesy wasn't one of them. I was expecting 'king.'

He wrapped one arm around my waist and the other up my back, completely supporting my body weight. I swayed lightly on my feet and he gripped a little harder. "I've got you," he whispered.

The strength came back to my body, and I pressed my whole self against him so hard he teetered on the stairs. "You didn't answer my question. Are you the king?"

His eyes flashed. "No baby." He swept me off my feet and into his arms. "I'm the fucking court jester."

I squealed and kicked my feet. "No, not the jester!" I slapped at his shoulders. He was heading to the lake. "Where are you taking me?"

He set me down on the path and slipped his hand into mine. "On our date m'lady." We followed the pathway to the lake, and I gasped when we got to the dock and *Calliope* was moored at the end.

He squeezed my hand. "You need to inspect my work. Floyd's got a rule that a boat has to pass the sunset cruise engine test before we release it to the owners." He pulled the keys out of his pocket and slipped them into my hand.

"She's all fixed?" I thought that it was going to take at least three days.

Dylan gave a light shrug. "I guess you rubbed your mechanic the right way."

The double entendre was rude – but his wry grin made up for it. "Oh, did I?"

It felt like Dylan and I had been walking hand in hand

and joking with each other forever – except for the butter-flies having a party in my stomach. We neared the main cottage and I pulled my hand from Dylan's. I didn't think the staff would talk about me, but if the house manager was onsite, her loyalties sat with my parents, not me – and strolling hand in hand, laughing like a hyena with the mechanic wasn't going to be easily explained.

"By the way, someone from the Yates Estate called today to check in on *Calliope*."

"Oh no," I whispered, weaving my fingers through Dylan's once we were hidden by the forest between the main cottage and the boathouse.

"Don't worry. I told Floyd to tell your family's secretary, or whatever her job is…"

"Estate Manager," I grumbled.

"Whatever." He rolled his eyes behind his sunglasses. "Floyd told your estate manager that it was routine mainte-nance. The boat is running like a top – your family will never know that you almost murdered their beloved woody."

This time it wasn't a naughty slip of the tongue. Woody was a Lake Casper colloquial term for any old wooden boat. All the old rich men sat around smoking cigars and talking about their woodies without cracking a smile. As a teenager, I had teased my dad for it, but he didn't care.

I was practically skipping as we reached the dock. "I didn't do it on purpose, so it couldn't be murder. I think it would be considered boatslaughter."

Dylan's laugh was throaty and guttural. "Do I dare let someone capable of boatslaughter captain *Calliope?*"

I kicked off my black topsiders at the same time Dylan kicked off his flip-flops. I pointed to his footwear, "Do they issue all of you guys a pair of these?"

"All you guys?" Dylan raised his eyebrows and hopped

into the boat. He held out his hand and helped me get settled in the captain's chair.

"Hockey players." I turned the key and the engine roared briefly before settling into a low purr.

Dylan slid into the seat next to me. "They issue them along with a pack of Spits and an Otters' hat."

"Spits?" The hockey world had its own language – one that I didn't speak. I knew that barn meant arena and biscuit meant puck, but that's as far as my hockey jargon went.

"I forgot that you didn't grow up around the game. Sunflower seeds. A lot of the guys switched over to sunflower seeds when chewing tobacco wasn't cool anymore."

"Was it ever?" I scrunched up my face. "What are you guys, cowboys in the old west?"

He waggled his brows at me over top of his sunglasses and put the Otters' hat on my head. "There, you're a third of the way there." I turned the hat backward and navigated the boat into the deeper water before pushing down the throttle. The powerful engine growled and echoed off the granite outcroppings until we entered the choppy whitecaps of the big open water in the middle of the lake.

As we rounded Danger Island, I slowed and followed the channel markers, keeping an eye on the rocks that had claimed the propellers of many boats.

"You're a good Captain." Dylan squeezed my hand but didn't let go.

There was no other way to describe how I felt with Dylan besides right. It felt both new and exciting, like a new relationship should feel, but also full of comfort and knowing, like we'd been together for twenty years and knew and loved each line and wrinkle and fault of the other. "You're a good mechanic." I patted the steering wheel. "She's running the best I've ever seen." I slipped my hand from his but was glad when he kept his resting on my thigh. I turned in my seat to look at the back of the boat and as a result, his hand naturally crept higher on my thigh. "And look…" I turned to face forward and crossed my legs, trapping his fingertips between my thighs, "no smoke."

"Always a good sign," he laughed. The setting sun reflected in his glasses.

Another boat passed and we both gave the friendly Lake Casper wave. The driver returned the wave and gaped at the boat. He was clearly appreciative of the rare woody. I glanced over at Dylan and could see that he was dealing with a woody of his own. That's when the guilt crept in. I was having so much fun with Dylan, but I knew that I wouldn't sleep with him. Was that fair to him? I mean, he was a hot-blooded man and I had first-hand knowledge of the power he wielded between his legs.

His eyes caught mine and he leaned over to kiss me on the cheek. "You look so hot with that hat on backward."

I took it off and put it on his head. "I think it looks better on you."

"I doubt it." He turned it backward and was easily the hottest-looking man I'd ever seen, his hair flicking out from beneath it. "The sun sure is giving us a show tonight. If we weren't on a secret date, I'd take you for an ice cream cone at Laketown Lickety."

The ice cream shop was accessible by both car and boat, and at this time of night would have a lineup down the road and the dock. "Mmmm. I could go for ice cream."

He grinned and pulled a cooler from the back of the boat. "I thought you might say that. It was either champagne or ice cream." He held up a bottle of champagne and two ice cream sandwiches.

"I'm a responsible boater." I patted the steering wheel, "I'll have one of the sandwiches. But if you want a bit of bubbly, I won't object."

"Bron," he unwrapped one of the ice cream sandwiches. "I don't know if you know this, but I had a bit of a rough patch a couple of years ago."

"I remember." I pulled back so the boat was barely in gear, and we rocked gently as the boat cruised along the shoreline at a snail's pace. "You stopped calling me for a while."

"I had some issues with booze and Coach stopped me before I hit rock bottom."

I knew that the timing fell within his grieving of his parent's death. "You're lucky to have him in your life. But Dylan, I wish you would've talked to me." I licked the edge of the ice cream sandwich and then squeezed his hand. "You could've talked to me about your parents."

"Could I?" He took a bit of his ice cream. "I thought that we were just…um…"

"Fucking?" I finished his sentence.

"Yeah." He shrugged. "I thought you got off on being with a dirtbag."

I finished the sandwich and licked the sticky wafer off my fingers. "Dylan Moss. I have never, ever been with a dirtbag."

"You know what I mean." He looked at the horizon.

"No, no I don't. I never saw you as anything but a hot guy who also made me laugh."

"That's not all I made you do." His lips turned up slightly. It had become very apparent that Dylan used humor to diffuse a situation and I wasn't going to fall into his trap.

"No. You're not getting out of that self-deprecating comment so easily. I wasn't slumming it with you, Dylan."

"Oh, come on." His head whipped to look at me. "You're telling me that you weren't just having some fun with someone completely disposable because that's how I felt."

Now I was getting angry. "I could say the same thing. You

showed up whenever you felt like it -sometimes at three a.m. Then I wouldn't hear from you for months at a time. You treated me like a summertime cottage girl, one that you'd never have to be serious about."

The boat rocked as we stared each other down. "That's not what I thought," he said quietly.

"Same." I crossed my arms across my chest. I could imagine walking down the aisle with Dylan Moss, even if it was forbidden by my parents. "I liked you for you."

He crossed his arms and his lips narrowed. "I liked you for you too."

It was a standoff of the weirdest complimentary argument I'd ever experienced. His lip quivered before mine. Once his laugh escaped his lips, mine did too. "Are we fighting about how we genuinely like and respect each other?" he laughed.

I took my sunglasses off and wiped a tear of laughter.

The lyrics to a Van Morrison song floated through the air and once I put the boat in neutral and turned off the engine, I was able to identify it – *Moondance*. The pinks and purples of the sunsets were reflecting off Dylan's glasses and the warm wind rustled my hair. "This song reminds me of my mom." He smiled and looked to the horizon.

"I wish that I could've met her. I can tell that you sincerely loved her." I paused. "Which is more than I can say for my mom."

"You're not close?" Dylan asked.

"Not at all. I was raised by nannies. My dad was always working, and my mom was either working out or going to some spa." As a kid, I was invisible to her, or more like a mosquito – an annoyance. As if on cue a mosquito's high-pitched whine droned by my ear.

"What about your dad?" Dylan turned to look at me and intertwined his fingers around mine.

"As I said, he worked a lot. Although, we had some things in common, like sailing."

"Your mom didn't like yachting?"

I laughed. "Oh, she liked yachting. I'm talking about racing dinghies. I'm not sure why they married actually." I partially knew the answer, my mom was with my dad for his money. My dad? I don't know what he got out of the deal.

An awkward pause followed. As the flute solo fluttered to an end, *Into the Mystic* came on the radio. "They must be doing a Van Morrison night," Dylan whispered. He stood and pulled me from my seat and slid his hand to my lower back and held my hand with his. I glanced around, scanning the horizon for boats.

"Don't worry, B," he whispered. "No one can see us." His breath was hot on my ear and to my surprise, Dylan started swaying and humming to the music. I was stiff as a board. Taking a test ride with the mechanic was explainable, dancing with him to the sunset? That was above and beyond the services offered at Lake Casper Marine. "Dance with me, B." This time he kissed my ear and I melted into him. Thankfully, he had a firm grip on my back. Holding onto his shoulder, I rested my head on his chest and let the music, waves, and breeze fill my body with their movement. Dylan and I were one, moving with nature and each other's gentle sway. I had to rethink this whole dating thing. As Dylan's heart thumped beneath my ear, I knew I'd never be able to let him go. I was falling in love. No. That wasn't true. I had completely and utterly fallen head over heels in love with Dylan Moss. And that meant one thing I was going to have to give up my fortune to be with him. At that moment, as the first stars started to appear, I was fully prepared to walk away from the Yates Petroleum dynasty for the man whose arms were wrapped around me.

And it felt good.

FOURTEEN
DYLAN

THE SWEAT ROLLED down my face and dripped from my chin. Leo barked orders and made us repeat the play.

"How many more times do we have to do this?" Mike raised his stick in the air. "It's perfect. That last time, totally perfect." His voice echoed through the barn.

"You were one stride behind," Leo shouted back and blew his whistle.

I skated up beside the assistant coach and my friend. "Leo, it was perfect. If you keep working these guys this hard, half of them are going to barf and the other half are going to collapse."

The sound of Jasper retching over the boards proved my point. Leo's lips had been drawn in a line, but they relaxed. "I just want them to do well."

"I know you do." I took off my glove and wiped the sweat from my chin. "But they're going to be no good to you if you keep pushing them this hard."

The buzzer sounded, but the guys continued the play. "Leo," I urged. "Come on."

He blew the whistle and the relief on the ice was notice-able. "You're right, Captain." He waved the guys off the ice. "Nice hustle today."

"Thanks." I didn't know if it was obvious, but I had given the practice at least one hundred and ten percent.

Leo followed me off the ice. "Moss," he called as he jogged on his skates to catch up to me before I went into the dressing room. "I meant to ask you, what's going on with you and the model? I noticed you two disappeared from Fitzy's boathouse the other night."

Leo and I had been friends for years. Would he know if I was lying? I was about to find out. "She wasn't feeling well. Something about gluten. I took her home."

"You two looked pretty cozy. I can't believe she'd be seen with a guy like you."

His comment was meant as a joke, but it cut like a blade. "We're just friends. I was helping her with her boat and invited her to come along, I don't think she knows too many people here."

"She doesn't know any normal people," Leo corrected. "She doesn't know any Laketownies."

I sighed. "True. But that's not her fault. And Leo, she's not a snob. She can hang out with anyone." I shot him a grin, "Even you."

He laughed, even though it could've been taken as an insult. "She does seem pretty cool for a billionaire. You should try to get in on that."

Billionaire. The word hit like a cross-check. I was barely a thousandaire. "In on what? Her, or her…" I hesitated, the word felt dirty, "billions."

Leo picked up on the bite in my voice. "Easy. It was a joke. And I thought you were just friends."

I paused with my hand on the dressing room door. "We

are just friends, and I don't let people talk shit about my friends, even if they are the assistant coach."

Leo pushed past me and into the dressing room. "I like this new fire, Moss. Whatever she is to you, keep doing it. It's working."

Was sexual frustration the key to playing well? There was that old wives' tale that some players were forbidden from having sex before a game, but it was something I'd never tried. Last night, just being within arm's reach of Bronwyn had gotten me rock hard. But we were dating now, going back to the way we should've started. She called it courting, I called it torture, but I secretly liked the buildup. When the time was right, thrusting into her warmth, those creamy thighs wrapped around me, was going to be fireworks, or something better than fireworks.

For now, I had to be content with dropping her off at her door with a kiss, squeezing her perfect ass, and going home to stroke one out, like I had done that morning– imagining her cherry red-lipsticked lips around my dick.

But it was more than sex. Even though those lips around my cock were a hard image to top. Imagining her sleepy eyes when they first opened in the morning, feeling her warmth in bed, making breakfast for her, all of these thoughts, were just as good as the dirty ones.

As I left the rink, my phone buzzed in my pocket. It was a text from Bronwyn, no words, just photos – the sunset from the night before and the selfie we'd taken. The sky looked like it was on fire behind us and both of us had the same smile on our faces. She looked radiant, the best I'd ever seen her – it was like she was glowing.

"Hey, Moss. You coming for carb-loading?" Mike shouted from his car.

I shoved my hockey bag in the back of the Volvo and

waved at the group of guys piling into Mike's truck. I wanted to go for pancakes at the crepe house. I wanted to take the day off and go wake surfing with Jasper and Tanner, I wanted to sneak into Bronwyn's bunkie and wake her up with a fancy coffee, but today I had an important reason for rushing to work. I was meeting a buyer.

The line of cars exiting the arena all turned towards downtown Laketown, but I turned right to head to the marina. My stomach probably couldn't have handled a stack of flapjacks, it was so tied up in knots. How much should I ask for the boat? I didn't want to just give it away, but I also didn't want to scare the buyer off with a high price tag. Just getting my original work out there would be advertising in itself, so maybe I should consider something lower – but I had thousands of dollars into the project, and it had taken me over a year to get her to where she sat today – almost finished.

As the thoughts swirled through my mind, I felt myself getting even more confused. I parked in the shade and dialed Floyd. When he didn't answer, I checked my watch – the buyer was scheduled to come in at seven-thirty – I had ten minutes to make up my mind.

"Shit," I muttered and scrolled through the boat buy and sell app on my phone. The prices were all across the map. I tapped my fingers on the steering wheel. The second person who could potentially help me out was probably sleeping. I debated for a minute and then pushed her contact number. As the phone rang, I couldn't help but smile.

"Mm... hello?" her voice was soft, and she definitely sounded like I had just woken her up. I could hear her sheets rustling in the background.

"Did I wake you up? I can call back later."

"It's okay." Her yawn was audible over the phone. "I

wanted to get up and go for a swim this morning anyway. What's going on? Is everything alright?"

Early morning phone calls were new in our relationship and I could see why there was concern in her voice. "Everything is totally fine. I wanted to ask your opinion about something."

"Sure." There was more rustling, and I imagined her sitting up in bed with her hair all over the place.

"Do you know anything about your dad's boat collection?"

There was a pause on the other end of the line. "Not really. I mean, what do you want to know?"

I had to tell her the reason I was calling, there was a hint of suspicion in her voice. "The other day when you were in the marina and you smudged the varnish on that wooden boat."

"Yeah…" Her voice went up at the end like she was asking a question.

"Well, that's mine. I designed it and have been building it from scratch over the years."

Her intake of breath was audible. "You made that boat? Dylan, it's beautiful."

My chest swelled. I had gotten other compliments over the years, but somehow, the words coming from her mouth meant more than anyone else's. "Thanks." I was glad that we were on the phone because the embarrassing redness in my cheeks was burning hot. "I have a potential buyer or two coming in to look at it today and I don't know what to charge."

Her voice sounded clearer, and I could hear the screen door opening in the background, she must have moved to the wicker furniture on her screened-in porch.

"Why are you selling it?" It wasn't the response I had

wanted. I didn't want to tell her the truth – I was selling it for the money. If I didn't have to sell it, I wouldn't.

"It's just a little project of mine – I had planned on selling it the whole time."

"And you didn't think of a price until now?"

"Um…" The temperature in the car was getting hot as the sun rose higher in the sky. "No, I mean. I was just doing it for fun. I just kind of thought that you might have some good advice for me. If I ask too much, they might not buy it. If I break even, it might still be a good deal, because people would see it at all of the shows. You know, it would get my name out there." I shut the car door and hurried to open up the marina before the buyer arrived, the phone squeezed between my neck and ear.

Her voice was confident but soft. "Don't you dare sell yourself short. I don't know how much your boat is worth, my dad's collection ranges from fifty thousand dollar boats up to well, *Calliope*."

"Right. Okay. I guess it's a hard question." My footsteps echoed through the empty bays, and I flicked on the lights by the security panel.

"Dylan. I'm going to give you one piece of advice. Well, maybe two pieces of advice."

I took a deep breath. "I'm ready. Shoot."

Her laugh was light and airy. "I'll give you my best slap-shot, that's a hockey thing, right?"

"I can take it." I laughed; she had a way of turning a serious conversation into something fun.

"What number would you be happy with?"

The varnish shone in the fluorescent lighting. My unnamed boat had beautiful lines and could potentially be iconic – especially if I was able to line up the v8 from one of the dealers. "Thirty thousand?"

"Is that a question?"

"Thirty thousand. I would be happy with that. It would cover my costs and give me a little profit."

"Alright—"

"Thanks, Bronwyn," I said quickly. A car had pulled into the parking lot, and I wanted to polish the hull before the buyer came in.

"I wasn't done."

"Oh. Sorry, about that." I grabbed a chamois and started to polish like the Karate kid.

"Alright, you're happy with thirty thousand."

"Mmhmm." I nodded even though she couldn't see me – and I knew better than to interject again.

"Ask ninety?"

"NINETY?" The phone slipped out from where I had it gripped between my shoulder and ear. My hand shot out and caught it before it smashed to the floor. "Did you say ninety?" I asked when I got the phone back in place.

"Yes. Here's your lesson for today. Rich people like expensive things. If you price it too low, they won't want it."

"But ninety. Bronwyn? It might be worth that from one of the big names, but I'm unknown. This is my first build."

"Good. That makes it even better. Trust me. Ask ninety."

The buzzer for the office door sounded through the building. "I've gotta go. He's here. Thanks, Bron."

"Good Luck, Mossy."

I slipped the phone into my pocket and rushed to the door, my heart hammering. Ninety thousand dollars. She was insane. I opened the door. The buyer was waiting, he was tall and looked to be in his fifties.

"Come on in." I held the door open for the man, wondering where I had seen him before – he looked very familiar. That happened a lot around here, there were so many celebrities and famous entrepreneurs, that a flash of recognition was usually followed by the realization that I had seen them on the pages of a magazine.

I held out my hand, "Dylan Moss."

The smile disappeared from the man's face and he seemed to recoil, but only for a split second. He cleared his throat and thrust out his hand. "Peter Yates."

FIFTEEN
BRONWYN

A MORNING PERSON. I never thought that I'd end up as one of those. But between making out like a teenager with Dylan and feeling like crap from the baby, I had gotten used to seeing the sunrise – and while Laketown sunsets were still one of the most spectacular displays in the world, her morning shows were almost as good.

Instead of running through my morning yoga practice, I spent the hour lying on my mat, watching the sky as it shifted from gray to pink to blue wondering what the hell I was going to do. My hands rested on my belly and traced the subtle line of a stretch mark. The salve that Dylan had gotten from Thelma had made my hands feel so incredible, I'd started rubbing it on my belly too.

As I made my way to the bunkie I noticed Minerva's car in the roundabout, along with the house manager's.

"Minerva?" My voice echoed through the great room of the main cottage.

Minerva appeared holding a dishtowel. "Yes, Miss."

"What's going on?"

"We're preparing for the arrival of Mr. Yates."

"Thanks, Minerva. When are they arriving?"

"It's just your father." A voice spoke from behind me.

"Dad." I turned and gave my father a hug. "I thought that you guys were going to be gone for a week or two."

My dad gave me a squeeze and then released me from the embrace. "Your mother has decided to stay in Vail for another week or so to…" He glanced behind me and whispered in my ear, "recover."

"I got it, Dad. And I'm pretty sure everyone knows what she does in Vail. You know, when she comes back with a new face."

He sighed. "I know, it's a bit much, isn't it? I always thought that she was the most beautiful years ago when I met her, with her original nose – the one you've never seen."

This was a side of my father I'd never seen before. I took a step back and realized that the lines beside his eyes were a little deeper, and there were dark circles under his eyes. Unlike my mother, he was aging, and he looked tired. But as a Yates, we didn't really do emotion or conversation deeper than the latest stock prices or events at the club. I wanted to ask him if he was okay, but "It's nice to see you, Dad," is what I said.

"Same, Bronnie," he smiled. "It's nice to be back at the estate. How are you doing? You look… good."

He looked at me as though he were seeing me for the first time.

"I'm doing fine, Dad."

"Do you want to go to the club for dinner?" His eyes glanced at my stomach, and I swore that he breathed out a sigh of relief that the beach ball wasn't there yet.

"Can we do it tomorrow? I have plans tonight."

"Plans?" His eyes narrowed.

The lie came out easily. "I'm going to hang out with my friend Jessie."

"Jessie?" He scrunched his brow. "Do I know this Jessie?"

I made my way to the door. "I don't think you've met her, she's away a lot training for the Olympics."

"The Olympics." He nodded his approval. "Maybe tomorrow then."

"Sure, Dad. Tomorrow." It seemed as though he needed to talk, but that's not what we did. As I walked to the bunkie, I made a promise to myself to put an effort in with my father. My mom was pretty much a lost cause, but I still felt as though there was a good person somewhere inside my dad.

I spent the day slathering cream on my body and imagining what it would be like to live in Laketown with a townie. Not on the shores of Lake Casper, but on a street in the town, in a small house where you wave at your neighbor in the morning and have a garden in the back yard. But what kind of a job could I get? I scrolled through my phone looking at college courses that could give me a skill, any skill that I could use to get a job in Laketown. If I was going to give up my fortune, I couldn't ask Dylan to take care of me and the baby. I Googled 'marina mechanic salary' and wondered what it would be like to live on between forty and eighty thousand dollars a year. I rubbed my hand on the down-filled sofa that cost ten thousand dollars – there definitely wouldn't be one of these in my future, that's for sure. But I kept going back to the photo of Dylan and me smiling together at sunset. The way I felt with him was better than the way I felt cooped up in this cage. That's when I knew that I could do it. I could give all of this up to be with Dylan. I could sit on a second-hand orange and brown plaid sofa and work whatever minimum wage job I could get.

Instead of dread, I felt excitement and wonder, like a flurry of butterflies had been released in my belly. There were three things I needed to do that day. One: to see if Jessie was going to the Otters versus Pros game that night and somehow invite myself to tag along. Two: figure out what the heck I could do to make a living in Laketown, and third: figure out how to keep seeing Dylan, now that my dad was back in town.

IT WASN'T INTENDED to be a disguise, but I would never have been seen in public with an Otters' baseball hat pulled low on my head, a baggy sweatshirt, and mom jeans.

"You're unrecognizable," Jessie laughed as I approached her in the parking lot. "I almost thought you were coming to rob me."

I looked down. "It's not that bad, is it?"

Jessie shoved me and laughed. For a small girl, she was a lot stronger than she looked and I took a step to the side and rubbed my arm theatrically. "You look super cute – and incognito."

"That's exactly what I was going for," I smiled. Jessie was also wearing a New York Thunder sweater over the top of leggings. "Is Kane excited to be playing against his old team?" We walked together into the rink. Immediately, I was jostled around by the crowd. Everywhere I looked was a sea of blue and white. Before Jessie could answer, I whispered, "I didn't think that there were this many people in Laketown."

Jessie laughed and hooked her arm in mine. "Everyone from Laketown and all the towns within one hundred miles come to these games. It's 'the' event of the summer."

"I thought 'the' event of the summer was the fundraiser at the Club."

"Maybe for your crew." Jessie tugged at my arm and we were like salmon swimming upstream through the crowd.

"Where are we going?" I asked.

That's when I heard the whispers around us and could see the fingers pointing. I'd been spotted. I put my head down and pressed into Jessie, hoping to avoid eye contact or worse, photographer's lenses. The bulbs flashed and I put my hand over my eyes. It had been so long since I'd been rushed by fans and photographers, I was out of practice at dodging them. To my surprise, Jessie had stopped in front of me, and photos and notepads were being thrust at her. That's when I realized, they weren't shouting my name – they were shouting Jessie's.

Peering between my fingers, I saw that none of the eyes were trained on me – they were all on Jessie. I put down my hands and while it was a foreign sensation, I stood back and enjoyed being overlooked. Jessie took photos with her fans and signed as many autographs as were books thrust at her. She waved at the crowd and then pulled me along behind her by my hand.

"Sorry about that," she shouted as we entered the main area of the arena.

"You're famous," I smiled and tried to keep from breathing hard as I followed the super-fit Olympian up the miles of stairs.

"It's a hockey town, but they make exceptions for figure skaters if you make it to the Olympics."

"I'd love to watch you skate someday."

Jessie led me down a hallway and into a private box. "Is this just for us?" I looked around at the empty seats.

"Yep." Jessie slipped into one of the reclining chairs and opened a bottle of sparkling water. I joined her and took a second bottle from the ice-filled bin of drinks.

"You can have champagne or beer if you'd like." Jessie took a sip of her drink. "My coach doesn't want me having any alcohol before the games."

Slowly sipping my sparkling water, I tried to formulate

an excuse. "I don't like to drink if I'm driving." It had been the same excuse I'd used all summer with my lake friends.

"I can drive you home if you'd like to have some."

"Thanks for the offer, Jessie, but I'm okay."

Jessie glanced at me before nodding and my heart felt like it stopped in my chest. Did she have some sort of female intuition telling her that I was lying? Oh, my God. I just realized that Jessie was going to be an aunt and she had no idea. My son or daughter was going to have an Olympian auntie and a National League hockey star uncle.

Even though my mind had been made up, I was telling Dylan about the baby, the realization that there was a potential entire new family that could take the place of my uppity, snooty one, felt comforting.

"Popcorn?" Jessie dug her hand into a bag and passed it to me.

"Is this on your athlete-approved list of foods?" I took a handful of the salty popcorn and popped a kernel into my mouth.

"Carbs." She grinned and crunched. "And Bronwyn, if you and Dylan ever decide to come clean about your relationship, you'll be invited to all of the public skating parties. I'll show you a few tricks."

My cheeks flushed pinker than the bottle of rosé in the bucket of ice beside us. "We're just friends."

"Mmmhmm. Sure." She spoke through a mouthful of popcorn. "I don't know you well, Bronwyn but I know that guy down there." She pointed to the ice where the players had started warming up. "And he's not fooling me."

"I can't skate." I tried to steer the conversation back to the public skating party nightmare.

Jessie choked on a piece of popcorn and pounded her chest with her fist. "Does Dylan know that? They pretty much issue every baby a pair of skates when they leave the hospital here. I don't know anyone who can't skate."

"I mean, I've gone in Central Park, but we just kind of stood there." It had been a photoshoot, and I wouldn't have called it skating, it was more like extra slippery, jerky walking and then trying to remain upright before being helped to the side.

Jessie handed the bag of popcorn to me. "Well, it's a good thing that you know a couple of people who can teach you a few things. I'll have you doing a waltz jump in no time."

The idea of gliding around the ice, hand in hand with Dylan, our friends skating around us seemed more like paradise than spending a week in the South of France. My hand had subconsciously found its way to rest on my belly and I watched Jessie's eyes as they traveled from my face to my hand.

With the fresh sheet of ice gleaming in the stadium lights, an excited murmur spread through the crowd. The announcer came over the loudspeakers and introduced the opposing team of the evening, the New York Thunder. The audience cheered and most stood on their feet. When Kane stepped onto the ice, Jessie hopped up and screamed and pumped both of her fists in the air. The admiration on her face shone and brought tears to mine. The diamond on her finger sparkled as she took her seat. After the final Thunder player had entered the stadium, the lights went down, and AC/DC blared through the speakers.

"Ladies and gentlemen. Your hometown Ooooooooooooooooootters." The announcer bellowed.

The excited crowd took it up a notch. If the fans were at a nine before, they were now at an eleven. The blue and white jerseys exploded from the boards through a sea of dry ice, and I found myself on my feet. Jessie smiled as she stood clapping beside me.

As the players were introduced, my heart was in my throat. My secret boyfriend was down there, and all these people were here to see him. "Where is he?" I leaned in to Jessie and yelled.

"He's the Captain, he'll be on last."

"He's the Captain?"

Jessie shot me a puzzled look. "He is, and look..." Jessie gestured with her thumb to the box beside us. "Scouts. Rumor has it they're here to watch Dylan again."

The pride bloomed across my chest. Dylan hadn't told me any of this. "Does Dylan know?"

Jessie rolled her eyes. "He shouldn't, but my big-mouth boyfriend told Leo. And everybody knows that guy can't keep a secret."

"I can't believe he didn't tell me," I said, more to myself.

Jessie elbowed me and raised her eyebrows, "Why would he tell you that? You're just friends."

"Jessie. I..."

The announcer interrupted me before I could tell Jessie the secret that had been burning me up inside. Dylan was my man, and I was about to give up everything to be with him.

"Captain of the Laketown Otters, Dylannnnnnnn Moss." My hands clenched in front of me like a little kid waiting for an ice cream cone.

Jessie hooted for Dylan and the rest of the auditorium chanted: Mossy, Mossy.

He burst through the cloud of dry ice and I heard a woo-hoo coming from my body.

After the puck dropped, I was enthralled. I had been to National League games before, but none had drawn me in and enraptured me like this game. The skating was fast, and the hits were hard.

"Who are you cheering for?" I leaned into Jessie and we both kept our gaze locked on the action.

"Don't tell Kane, but I grew up cheering for the Otters, it's in my DNA to root for the hometown team. If Dylan plays his cards right, this could be his ticket out of here and away from fixing boats for a living.

How could I have been so short-sighted? I kept my eyes glued to the action, but my mind was racing. I had sold Dylan short, not only to my parents but to myself. Dylan was talented, smart, and good-looking, He could do anything he put his mind to – especially with the right person backing him. A good woman standing by his side supporting him, not hiding him from her parents. Not being embarrassed by his job or his blue-collar upbringing.

"You okay?" Jessie's voice brought me out of my daydream.

I blinked hard and the sounds of the crowd and the bangs of the boards with body checks came back into focus. "I'm fine." I gave her one of my cover-perfected smiles.

"Good." She patted my arm.

The crowd erupted in cheers and the red goal light flashed above the Thunder's goalie. Jessie and I whipped our heads back to the game. The first goal of the game had been scored by my boyfriend. He was gliding on one skate, his stick in the air, and his eyes – his eyes were on mine. I leaped out of my seat and clapped, holding his gaze until his team members surrounded him.

"Jess. I…I need to tell you something."

She took her eyes from the game and trained them on mine. "What is it?"

"I'm in love with your brother." The words spilled out of my mouth.

"I know." She gave me a hug. "I think he knows, but you should probably be telling him that."

My cheeks hurt as I tried to keep the grin from spreading across my face, "I'm going to tonight."

SIXTEEN

DYLAN

Just knowing that Bronwyn had been in the barn had made me play better. It wasn't to impress her; it was as though her presence somehow made everything – right. Was I losing my mind? I didn't have any worries when she was around, and for the first time in a long time, I could focus on the game.

"Nice work tonight, Moss." Leo clapped me on my back as we left through the players' entrance. "What's your secret?" There was a gleam in his eye. And I knew that he was waiting for me to say something really dirty. Old me totally would have made some immature comment, but I felt protective of Bronwyn like she deserved more respect than locker room banter.

"It's not what you think." I pushed open the metal door and humidity hung thick in the air. "It's literally the opposite of what you think."

Leo stopped so quickly his running shoes squeaked on the pavement. "The opposite? Who are you and what have you done with Dylan Moss?" he laughed.

"We're taking things slowly." I tossed my bag into the back of the car and let the hatchback click shut. "And Leo," I whispered. "The pent-up energy – it's making me play better, I swear."

"That old wives' tale?" Leo continued to the lobby where his girlfriend, Faith would be waiting along with my girl. I jogged to catch up to him.

"I think there's something to it." I grabbed onto Leo's forearm, pulling him to a stop. "I'm not even jerking off," I whispered.

"Dude." Leo wrenched his arm free. "Too much information."

It was standard locker talk, but maybe we were both growing up. I shrugged. "You asked."

Leo laughed and opened the door to the lobby. "True enough. Well, whatever you're doing – or not doing, keep not doing it. We won tonight, but not by much. And man, that first goal was a beauty. Now, are you ready for the fans?"

The rest of the team had already joined the National League players in the lobby. It was a Laketown tradition that the players would hang out in the lobby after the games and hand out autographs. It was good to see that the National guys were playing along too. The Laketown kids were going to remember this series for years.

After signing what felt like a hundred autographs and posing for double the number of photos, I was spent.

"Can I have your autograph?" A girl wearing an Otters hat and frumpy baggy grandma clothes thrust a wrinkled gas receipt and a pen at me.

I took the pen. "Who should I make it out to?"

The giggle made me look up. It was Bronwyn, in disguise.

"How about you make it out to your not secret girlfriend."

Instead of signing the paper, I wrapped my arm around her neck and pulled her ear close to my mouth. "For real? What about the paparazzi?" I hadn't truly understood her rationale for keeping the relationship a secret, but hell, I hadn't cared. Secret or not, I was with Bronwyn Yates.

"Fuck the paps." She took off the baseball hat and her eyes sparkled almost as brightly as her white-blonde hair. Only Bronwyn could look gorgeous under fluorescent lighting.

I kissed her cheek and she folded against me. I wrapped my other arm around her shoulder as we kissed, the gasps of recognition disappearing into the background. When her lips left mine, the world came back into view along with ten million cell phones – all pointing at us.

"I guess the cat's out of the bag," I whispered into her ear. She slid her arm around my waist.

"Good."

I don't know what was better, walking out of the arena with a short-handed goal against the New York Thunder under my belt or, having the most beautiful woman I'd ever known on my arm. The crowd followed us outside and a familiar luxury SUV pulled up in front of us.

The tinted window rolled down. "What are you looking at? Get in," Jessie shouted.

I opened the door for Bronwyn, and she slipped across the leather seat as I shut the door behind me. Kane eased his way through the crowd. "I thought we had it bad." Kane looked in the rearview mirror. "But you, Bronwyn, that's another level of craziness."

"I know," she sighed. "And that wasn't even that bad."

Kane navigated the Mercedes to Oak Street. "Are you two coming to the after-party?"

I looked at Bronwyn and she shook her head subtly, and her eyes told me that she was looking to do something other than hanging out with a bunch of hockey players – and her hand sliding to the front of my jeans confirmed it. "I'm actually trying to stay away from parties right now – Coach's orders. But...if you want to go..."

"You know what. That sounds like fun, but I'm very tired." She spoke through a very convincing yawn.

Kane glanced in the rearview mirror. "So, I'll drop you two off at the Yates Estate then?"

"Sure--" I looked to Bronwyn as I answered but she interrupted me.

"No." Her voice was stern and then softened. "I mean, I'd really like to see your house."

If it wasn't dark, she would've been able to see the wrinkles in my forehead. In all the years that we'd been together, we'd never gone to my house. I racked my brain trying to remember if I'd put the dirty dishes in the dishwasher and if I'd put away, or even folded the baskets of laundry that had piled up in my room. I was a bachelor working a full-time job and training in elite hockey, I didn't have time to fold my boxers up into squares.

"I'd like to see the flower gardens. You know, like from the bouquet you brought me the other day."

Jessie spoke from the passenger seat. "The gardens are beautiful."

"Alright then, let's go to my house." It seemed weird, but with the added pressure from my cock pressing against the buttons on my jeans, I didn't care if we were going to a shack in the woods.

THE LIGHTS from Kane's SUV hadn't even left the driveway when Bronwyn came at me. As soon as the front door was shut and she pressed me up against it, her fingers fumbling at the button on my jeans.

"What happened to taking it slow?"

She paused and looked up at me then nipped at my bottom lip. "Maybe I'm just teasing you."

I arched my back pushing my hips and buttons harder into her fingers. "Do your best. It's making me play better than I ever have in my life."

"Really?"

"Really." My cock was throbbing and there was no way I wanted her to stop – but we'd had a deal, and even though I said I wasn't superstitious, what if the blue balls were the secret to my hockey success?

She traced the bulge in my jeans with her nail and slid down my body to her knees. The heat from her breath filtered through the denim and goosebumps erupted over my entire body. My knees almost buckled when she kissed the zipper. In this state, if she were to take me in her mouth, I was a goner.

The sparkle in her eyes as she looked up at me made my legs feel even weaker. I let my hands rest on her silky hair. "What did I do to deserve this?" I meant her, not the teasing, but she misunderstood and rose to kiss me again.

"That goal. I've never been with a hockey star before." I let the comment slide, we'd never spoken about our pasts, but I was pretty sure there had to be a few pro players under her designer belt.

I scooped her up in my arms and took the stairs two at a time and tossed her onto my bed. I breathed a sigh of relief when I saw that I had made it that morning and her hair was splayed out over the plaid comforter. I crawled over the top of her and kissed her jawbone, her breath was raspy against my ear. "I've never been with a supermodel before."

She laughed and slapped at my arm. "That's not true. You've been with me before."

I tapped my chin like a detective from an old movie. "Well, you've got me there, Princess."

She crossed her arms across her chest and gave me a fake-looking pout. "What happened to Queen?"

"They behead people who do stuff like this to the Queen."

"Stuff like what? —"

Instead of responding, I undid the button on her ugly jeans and she wriggled to help me as I slid them down her mile-long, tanned legs.

"This." I kissed the front of her panties, and she squeezed her knees around my ears.

"Dylan, wait." Her voice was breathy as I bit the pink fabric and pulled the panties down with my teeth. She put the panties back in place. "Wait a minute."

I rested my chin on the bone between her legs and stared up at her.

"Not like that. Come up here." It was getting really weird, her words were serious, but her voice was filled with giggles.

"My Queen." I bit the panties again. "Permission to pause the talk, wait until after I've…" I was going to say eaten, but it seemed too crass. Instead, I kissed one thigh then the other.

Her legs trembled against my head and her fingertips had made their way to my hair. "Permission granted."

It took everything I had not to kick off my 501s and fuck her. My brain was into our dating game, but my cock was clearly not on board. He didn't care about the hockey, or the build-up anymore. He wanted some action.

Bronwyn writhed underneath my face, arching her back and moaning. "I'm getting close, Moss. I'm going to…" Her back was arched tight like a bow and my comforter was fisted in her hands. "Come." She screamed as her body bucked beneath me. She was twitching as I replaced her panties, and she flinched as I patted the front of the floral lace into place. She was breathing heavily, her chest rising and falling sharply as I kissed my way up her body.

I propped myself up on my elbow and pressed my body against hers. There was no way she'd be able to miss the raging hard-on pressing into her hip. "What did you want to talk about my Queen"? I was hoping it was an amendment to our agreement.

She propped herself up on her elbows. "I don't want our relationship to be a secret anymore."

I nodded. "I figured as much when you let ten thousand people photograph us together tonight." I brushed her hair behind her ear. "That felt good by the way."

"Didn't it?" She smiled and nuzzled her face into my chest.

"Alright, so we're official? You're my girlfriend." I couldn't believe that this was happening to me.

She batted her eyelashes at me. "If you'll have me."

I threw myself on her and her giggle in my ear made my heart soar. The feeling at that moment was better than any goal I had ever scored. I went to kiss her, but she put her finger on my lips. "There's one more thing."

"Anything." Was this where we changed the rules? I didn't think it was possible for my cock to get any harder, but it proved me wrong. I shifted uncomfortably, my fingers twitching to release the throbbing monster from my jeans, like a gunfighter in the countdown to a duel.

"It's a weird question. And I don't want you to take it the wrong way."

This was definitely not the direction I thought the conversation was headed and my tense body relaxed. "You can ask me anything, Bron."

She opened her mouth, and a little squeak came out like her throat had closed around her words.

"What is it?" I had never seen her like this. Something was wrong.

She sat up completely and I wrapped my arm over her shoulders.

She took a deep breath and cleared her throat. "Would

you still want to be my boyfriend if I didn't have any money?"

My head jerked involuntarily like I'd been slapped. "What? What are you talking about?"

She stared at her fingers in her lap. "If I lost everything, would you still be interested in me?"

I shifted, so I could slip my hand under her chin and force her to look me in the eye. "Bron? What kind of a question is that? Do you think I'm with you for your money?"

"No," she gushed. "Not at all. It's just something I wanted to ask you."

"Are you alright? Is everything okay?"

"I'm fine, Dylan. I really am. It's just… my family. They put these ideas into my head about every man."

"Every man, or just the dirty mechanic who fixes their boats?" I narrowed my eyes at her. Like a bad third period, this night had taken a turn for the worse.

"It's not like that." She moved closer to me, but I inched back.

"Yeah, it isn't like that. I can't believe you would even ask me a question like that. But yes, Brownyn. If in some parallel universe you lost all your money, I would still be in love with you."

Her eyes shot open wide, and I clamped my mouth shut, but the words were out. I took her hand in mine. "If you worked the night shift at the grocery store and lived year-round in Laketown, I would still love you. You would still be the kindest, sweetest, and most interesting person on the planet. Not to mention beautiful. You're the most beautiful person I've ever met, inside and outside. You never looked at me like I was a Laketownie. You never treated me any differently. Until tonight.

Her eyes shimmered. "Dylan. I love you." She slipped her

hand into mine. We had just declared our love to each other, so why did it feel so sad.

"Come on." I pulled the comforter and sheets up and she crawled underneath. I handed her one of my Otters T-shirts and she changed into that from her sweater. I took off my shirt and slipped into the bed behind her and pulled her body close to mine, wrapping my arms around her tightly. Her breath slowed into her sleep tempo, but I couldn't sleep. Why did she have to ask me that question? I had never thought about her money. But her family obviously did. I kissed her ear. "I love you, Bron."

Deep down I knew it wasn't coming from her, but all the pieces seemed to fall into place. She wasn't hiding me from the paparazzi. She was hiding me from her family – and now that we were official, she was going to have to prove to them that I wasn't a gold digger.

That wasn't her job. I would prove it to them myself.

SEVENTEEN
BRONWYN

As the room came into focus, it took me a second to figure out where I was. A Wayne Gretzky poster was on the wall above me, and I was wrapped in a very masculine-looking plaid comforter.

Dylan. I was at Dylan's house. I rolled over to snuggle into him but was met with an empty bed. "Dylan?" The house was silent. I pulled back the curtain and saw that the sun had just crested the horizon and a pink hue hung over the wartime bungalows on Dylan's street.

I unwrapped myself from the covers and tiptoed to the bathroom. It was empty, so I splashed some water on my face and went downstairs. The house was cute but still felt like a parent's house. The furniture was old and time-yellowed family photos hung on the walls. I laughed as I fingered the lace curtains – they definitely weren't Dylan's style. I poured myself a glass of water and looked out the kitchen window, where a garden full of the same beautiful pink flowers that Dylan brought me ran along the entire length of the fence.

"Dylan?" I walked around the entire house and even opened the front door to see if he was sitting on the porch.

My heart rate increased a few beats for every passing minute. Where had he gone? He had been upset the night before. I shouldn't have asked him about the money. Dammit. I knew the answer. He didn't care about the money. My mother had put that idea into my head, and I didn't know why I had brought it up. Except for the fact that when I told my family about Dylan, I was going to be homeless and penniless.

I sat on the porch swing and rocked it lightly as I thought about my next move. I'd have to call one of the staff to come and get me. But I didn't want to leave before I told Dylan about the inheritance. I took a sip of water and gulped it down. After that was over, I'd have to tell him about the next big thing – the baby.

Baby steps. I whispered to myself and then shook my head at the absurdity of it all.

I don't know how long I sat on the porch swing before a set of headlights turned down the street.

"Where have you been?" I asked.

Dylan got out of the car and joined me on the swing. "I had to go get the vulva," he said.

"The what?" I must've heard wrong.

Dylan chuckled. "It's the nickname for my car. The Volvo." A line of crimson spread along his stubbled jawline.

"I guess it makes sense, but real mature." I gave him a laugh to know that I was joking. The rusty car in front of me looked like it had seen better days.

He gave a half-hearted shrug at the immature comment. "You looked so peaceful sleeping this morning I didn't want to wake you up, but I didn't think you'd want a motorcycle ride home."

He was right. "I thought you'd abandoned me here." I snuggled into him as the sun rose higher over the horizon and handed him the glass of water. "Need a drink?"

"I'd never abandon you, Bron." He took a sip and then kissed me on the cheek with his cold lips. "But…" he glanced at his watch, "…there are a few things I need to do this morning."

"I can't believe I forgot to ask. What happened with the boat buyer?"

Dylan took a deep breath and open his mouth like he was about to speak but then changed his mind. "I'm not sure that he's interested. We didn't even discuss the price."

I put my hand on his arm. "It's a beautiful boat, Dylan. I think you're going to be surprised with how many people are going to want your work."

"Thanks, Bron. That means a lot coming from you." He rubbed the back of his neck. "It's a bit of a relief though. I think I might want to keep this one for myself."

Dylan stood and pulled me from the swing. I threaded my fingers behind his neck and kissed him. "Do you want to help me get dressed?" I gave him a wry smile and a little wink.

"Oh, man," he groaned. "I would love that, but this is very important."

"Getting undressed is more fun anyway." I gave him another wink. Dylan didn't follow me into the house, and I dressed quickly and ran out the front door to where he was waiting in the car.

"Don't you have to lock the door?" I asked, as I tried to open the passenger door. The handle clanked in my hand, but the door didn't budge. Dylan reached across and opened the door from the inside, and I slid into the passenger seat.

"I don't have keys for the house." I pressed the button to roll up the window and it shuddered and then didn't go up at all.

"The window doesn't work either."

"That's okay. I could use some fresh air." I shot him a smile and tried to relax. The air in the car felt comfortable but also strained. I wondered if I could be reading too much to it and was projecting my guilt onto him. I should've told him everything.

The car belched a trail of dark smoke as we headed through town. There was no sign of life on the main street except for a light on in the local bakery and coffee shop.

"Would you like a coffee?" Dylan asked. "I should've made some before I got up this morning. What kind of a host am I?" He shook his head.

Coffee. One of the few things from my past life that I truly missed. "I'll get some when I get home," I smiled and patted his leg. "I don't want you to be late for whatever it is that you have to do."

"Thanks, Bronwyn." The car shuddered as he pressed down on the gas, and we headed out of town toward my cottage. We didn't talk much on the drive and at one point Dylan turned up the radio. It was tuned into one of the two local stations, the country station.

"This is a pretty song." I had never really listened to country music, and it caught me by surprise that the lyrics were so beautiful.

"Well, it's debatable if that's country. But yes. It is pretty." He gave me a wry grin. "If you're a chick."

And just like that, we were back to joking. With the music in the background, I tried to figure out how I was going to explain to my family why Dylan had dropped me off.

"I'm sorry about last night." I turned the radio down.

Dylan didn't take his eyes from the road. "It's okay, Bron. I think I know where that was coming from. And just so you know, even if you were broke, I would dedicate every waking moment to making your life as happy as it could be."

Tears sprang to my eyes. Dylan was already working two jobs to support himself. I swiped at the tears hoping that he hadn't noticed. Maybe this was a bad idea. I couldn't ask him to take care of me. That's when it dawned on me, I didn't care about losing my fortune. I could drive around in this crappy car, I could work at any job, but what I couldn't do, is ruin this beautiful man's life beside me. Plumes of dust rolled behind us as we wound our way down the winding trail to the estate.

"Hey, Dylan. I'm actually in the mood for a walk. Do you mind letting me out here?" We were about a mile away from the estate.

"Are you sure?" He slowed the car and looked at me with raised eyebrows.

I gave him a big smile. "Yes, babe, I'm sure."

"Oookay." He stopped the car and put it in park. "I didn't know that you liked walking."

"There's a lot you don't know about me, Dylan Moss." I tried to be playful about it. "And one of those things is that I love walking." I didn't.

Dylan reached across me to open the door. "I'd do it from the outside, like a gentleman, but..." he shrugged. "You know."

I pushed the door open. Dylan ran to help me out of the car, and I let my hand linger in his. "Do you have a game tonight?" I asked.

"Nope." He rubbed the back of my hand with his. "Wow. Your hands feel incredible."

"It's that cream from Thelma. It's amazing. I've ordered more."

"You went through that jar pretty fast. Are you sure you're not part alligator?"

I wanted to tell him that most of it was being slathered over my belly and thighs, but I was second-guessing all of my life choices at that moment.

Dylan slipped his arms around my waist. "Don't worry

about anything, babe. I can see it in your eyes. It takes a lot more than a money comment to hurt my feelings."

I squeezed my eyes tightly to stop the tears. "I'm so sorry about that, Dylan. I really and truly am."

"I know." He kissed me and then stepped back but kept my hand in his. "I don't have a game or practice tonight. Do you want to go on a date? Maybe even the fishing one that we talked about?"

Yes. Everything in my body wanted to scream yes - to a fishing date. Who had I become? "I'll call you later." It wasn't a yes, but it wasn't a no. I hugged him and squeezed his perfect hockey player ass. I still didn't know what I was going to do. I had been so certain that giving up my fortune for Dylan was the right thing for me that I'd forgotten to think about him.

Disappointment flashed in his eyes and then he shot me his patented Dylan Moss smile. "I'll let you use my rod."

The man had a way of breaking the tension and I couldn't stop the smile from spreading across my face. "Can't wait." I stood on my toes, so we were eye to eye. "I love you, Dylan." I kissed him and gave his ass one more, maybe last, squeeze.

"I love you too, Bron. Enjoy your walk and message me when you get home." He kissed my hands.

I gave him a wave, then set off down the road - hoping to hell that nobody had seen my early morning walk of shame return to the bunkie.

EIGHTEEN
DYLAN

The vintage Ferrari was already parked outside the marina. He had beat me there.

"Shit." The gravel crunched under my work boots as I approached the door. "Were you waiting, long sir?"

Mr. Yates turned to look at me with absolutely no expression on his face. "No. Just a couple of minutes."

"Let me open up and turn off the alarm. Wait here one second." My heart was hammering against my ribcage – harder than it did after any hockey drills. While Bronwyn's dad wasn't exactly rude, he wasn't warm and fuzzy either. My fingers shook as I punched in the code for the alarm. Before I returned to the door, I took a deep breath. So many things were riding on this meeting. My life could take a dramatic turn, for the better or worse.

The metal door clanged as I opened it for Mr. Yates. "Come on in." It wasn't even seven in the morning, and he was dressed impeccably. His top sider loafers didn't make a sound on the concrete as he followed me to the almost completed boat.

He ran his finger down the gunwale and asked me a few

questions about the engine. "Do you want to see it? I've got it out back, it just needs to be cleaned up."

"I know that engine." He smiled. "And I know that Floyd's the best mechanic in the state."

For the first time, it seemed as though the smile on Mr. Yates' face was genuine. He studied every inch of the boat, stepping back every so often to look at her from further away. "You are a talented man. Mr. Moss. Where did you learn how to do this?"

The last meeting had been all business and the pleasantry caught me off guard. "M-m-my Dad," I stammered. I cleared my throat, "My father. He was a boat builder for the Watchrye Company."

Mr. Yates nodded and seemed to be listening but didn't take his eyes off the boat. "That's a great company." He did one more lap around the boat. "I usually wouldn't buy a boat without seeing her in the water, but I'm going to go with my gut on this one. Knowing that your father built for Watchrye, you've just sealed the deal."

"Sir?"

Mr. Yates pulled a piece of paper from his pocket and handed it to me.

"What is this?" I asked.

The chuckle was light and not condescending. "It's a bank draft."

I unfolded the piece of paper and dropped it when I saw the number printed on it.

Eighty thousand dollars.

"Don't lose that." He stepped on the corner of the paper with his shoe, and I reached to pick it up. "When will you be able to finish the boat?"

My hands were shaking, but I tried to play it cool and folded the draft, then stuffed it in the pocket of my mechanic's shirt. "As soon as Floyd has some time to help me with the engine."

The displeasure was obvious on his face, and he folded his arms across his chest. "You've got eighty thousand dollars in your pocket there, son. You'll get the last ten when it's completed – but I'd appreciate an actual date."

"Right." It was nearing the end of August. After Labor Day and before Thanksgiving, the pace at the marina slowed down a little. I met Mr. Yates' steely stare and knew that I had to pick a date and make that date work.

"October first." My voice sounded a lot more confident out loud than it did in my head.

Mr. Yates gave a nod. "That works for me, but I know how things work here in Laketown. You people don't have the same sense of urgency and respect for deadlines as the rest of the world."

It wasn't a new sentiment; things did happen at a slower pace in Laketown – it was a running joke that there was a separate time when you were in Laketown. There was 'regular' time, and then the slower version, the 'it will happen when it happens' Laketown time.

"October first. She'll be delivered to your dock." I extended my hand. He raised his eyebrow and then shook it.

"October first it is. It's been a pleasure doing business with you."

While I was trying to get the nerve up to say what I had to say, he stopped and turned. "Do you know my daughter, Bronwyn Yates? I believe she's used the water taxi service here."

Oh fuck. It was now or never.

"I do know her. Your daughter."

Mr. Yates put his hands on his hips. "Have you two spent any time together this summer?"

Things were getting weird. Could this have anything to

do with Bronwyn's weird question about money the night before?

"Actually, Mr. Yates. There's something I wanted to talk to you about."

He crossed his arms and met me with a narrowed gaze. "And what might that be?"

This was a lot harder than I had imagined in my rehearsal. "I've known your daughter for a few years now. And in that time we've gotten…"

I rubbed the back of my neck, trying to find the right words. This was the man's daughter.

"You've gotten what?"

I gulped. "Close."

"I see." His eyes looked so cold as if he could turn the marina into an icebox.

I shivered but squared my shoulders and met his icy eyes. "I want to ask your permission."

"My permission?" His eyebrows rose so high they almost met his salt and pepper hairline. "For what?"

"Mr. Yates, I've fallen in love with your daughter, and I would like your permission to date her."

You could've heard the tiniest engine part drop in the silence of the workshop. Mr. Yates' laugh broke that silence. "You. The mechanic. Want permission to 'date' my daughter?" He said it like it was a dirty word.

"Court?"

"Court my daughter? I don't think you have an understanding of what that means."

I was lost for words. "Mr. Yates, I love your daughter."

"Correction." He took a step toward me with his hands balled in a fist and I waited for the punch to the face. I tried not to wince as I saw the fist coming toward my face, but instead of the sting of a punch to the cheekbone, Mr. Yates plucked the bank draft from my pocket.

"No deal." He tucked the draft into his pocket.

He hadn't physically hit me, but I felt like the wind had been knocked out of me. "Sir?"

I had to fight for her. I jogged to him and grabbed his arm. He ripped it from my grip like my hand was made of flames. "Don't you ever touch me. And don't you ever…." He shook his finger in my face. "Touch my daughter, ever again."

NINETEEN
BRONWYN

Do pregnant women sweat more than regular women? I wiped my brow as I reached the estate. Luckily, I hadn't run into anyone and was able to slip into my bunkie undetected. I peeled out of my clothes from the night before and into one of my Italian one-piece bathing suits and silk cover-up.

As I passed the estate, I noticed that there was a lot of activity inside. The lights were on in my grandmother's wing, and I could see the staff, in their old-fashioned maid's outfits – my grandma was a traditionalist - airing out the quilts and polishing the furniture.

Great. Just what I needed; the matriarch was coming to town. As I passed the windows of the boathouse, I was happy to see that I looked the same. Although, my days of having a flat stomach were numbered and I wondered when I was going to start showing. Thelma still hadn't spilled the secret ingredient to her cream, but I planned to hound her until she either made me some more or told me how to do it.

The cool water felt good after my morning hike, and I let the sun dry me completely before I left the dock. Through the windows of the boathouse, I could see *Calliope* moored in her slip – thanks to Dylan. I smiled as I thought of him, but it turned to a sigh. What was I going to do? I had to talk to someone, but who? My mother was the worst choice out of everyone. My dad could be reasonable, but I didn't know whether he cared more about money, or me. Tess was my friend, but she was also a gossip.

I held my sandals as I walked barefoot to the bunkie. I couldn't have brought Dylan home for two reasons – one my dad was in town, and two, Dylan would see the nursery.

"Did you have a nice swim?" Lisa asked as I walked into the kitchen. She handed me a glass of sparkling water with freshly squeezed lemon.

"It was great. I love to swim first thing in the morning."

"I'm sure it feels great." Lisa started dropping frozen fruit and protein powder into the blender. "Any requests for a smoothie this morning?"

"It looks perfect the way you've got it." I pointed to the blender. "Make one for yourself too, while you're at it." I realized that sounded like an order. "If you'd like one," I added with a nervous laugh. "Lisa. Do you want to swim here? I don't mind if you go to the lake on your breaks."

"Thank you, Bronwyn. I will take the smoothie, but I'll swim on my own time."

I realized that even though I treated her well, I treated her like the help – and I didn't like that. "Here." I took the blender from her hand and poured two glasses of the thick green sludge.

"Where are the metal straws?" I asked.

Lisa opened one of the drawers and dropped a reusable straw into each of the smoothies. I handed one to her and grabbed her free hand. "You're on the clock. We're drinking these on the dock."

"But…" she resisted.

"No, buts. Lisa. Part of your job description now includes hanging out with me and being treated like a real person."

"But…" Her voice was quiet. "Would you order someone to hang out with you?"

She was so right, and I felt my face flush red. "I'm so sorry. I'm not myself, Lisa. I would like it if you would join me to sit and enjoy these smoothies. It's not an order and you don't have to do it. But it would mean a lot to me if you would."

She smiled. "As long as I'm still on the clock."

"Sassy." I gave her a little hip check. "I like this side of you."

"Be careful what you wish for, Miss Bronwyn."

I laughed and the two of us sat on the front porch. For the first couple of minutes, it was silent, and we listened to the loons. More of my grandmother's staff arrived and soon the noise from the main building had drowned out the sounds of nature. "Do you know when my grandmother is scheduled to arrive?" I asked.

"I don't know exactly." I'd have to check with the house manager. Lisa pointed to the main house with her straw. "But judging by the activity there, I wouldn't be surprised if the private jet is already in the air."

The smoothie was thick and almost tasted good. "Did you add spirulina to this?" I asked and jabbed at some of the green bits.

"I did. That stuff is pretty gross." She smiled and there were bits of green on her teeth.

"Does my mouth look like yours?" I bared my teeth at her.

"Oh, God. I hope not," she laughed and rubbed at her teeth with her finger. This moment with my housekeeper felt more real than any I'd had the entire summer I'd spent with Tess.

"Lisa, can I ask you something?"

"Of course, Bronwyn." She slurped up the last of the smoothie and set the glass on the nautical-themed coaster.

"Actually. I want to confess something, but I need you to promise to keep it a secret."

Lisa's eyes grew wide. "Do you need me to sign something? I already signed an NDA about the pregnancy and nursery and stuff."

"No. I just need your word."

"You've got it, Miss Bronwyn. As long as you haven't murdered someone."

This new side of Lisa was entertaining but caught me off guard so it took me a minute to reply.

"You haven't… murdered someone, have you?" she filled the dead air space.

I almost spit my last sip of smoothie back into the cup. "No. At least not yet," I laughed. "I do have a problem though, and I don't know what to do about it."

Lisa turned to face me, resting her arm on the back of the wicker sofa. "And you want advice from me?"

"Yeah," I nodded. "I do." Lisa seemed like one of the few level-headed people in my life – and she was a Laketownie. Maybe she could offer me a perspective I couldn't see.

"Okay then." She rubbed my arm briefly and then waited for me to get up the nerve to speak.

I took a deep breath. "Do you know Dylan Moss?"

She nodded. "Everyone knows Dylan Moss."

Of course, they did.

"Is he?" she pointed to my belly.

I nodded. "He is."

"Oh, my God." She put her hand to her mouth.

"Don't be so dramatic. You had to know that we've been fooling around over the years."

"There were rumors." She gave a light shrug.

"Well, there are going to be more rumors. We were photographed at the game last night."

"Bronwyn," Lisa gasped. "Your parents. They'll murder you."

"I know." I set the glass down on a coaster and curled my legs up underneath me. "Lisa. I love him. I'm in love with Dylan Moss." It felt good to say it to someone.

"But your parents…"

"I know. We have been seeing each other but keeping it a secret. Until last night. I decided…" my voice cracked. "I decided to give up all of this…" I gestured to the bunkie and the lake view. "My inheritance, for him."

"Wow." Lisa folded her hands in her lap. "Does he know?"

"Does he know that I have to give up my inheritance to be with him? Or does he know that I'm pregnant with his baby?"

"I guess both?"

I sighed. "He doesn't know either of those things and Lisa, I don't know if I can put all of that on him."

Her brow knitted. "Put all of what on him?"

This was going to be the hard part. "What can I offer? I don't have any skills, I spent all of my modeling money, my inheritance is the only thing I've got going for me. Dylan. He's just scraping by. I can't just dump a baby mama and a baby on a mechanic. That would ruin his life." Tears welled in my eyes and Lisa got up and walked away.

"Lisa?"

She returned with a box of tissues and sat down. "I see," she said. "Bronwyn, can I tell you what I honestly think? Without getting fired?"

"Lisa, you can tell me that I'm the worst person you've ever met."

She smiled. "Well, you're not the worst. That honor goes to your mother."

This wasn't what I was expecting, and it made me laugh. "True enough. And, I promise, I won't fire you."

She took a deep breath and pulled her brown hair into a loose bun. "I can't tell you what to do, Bronwyn. I really can't. But Dylan Moss. If you don't tell him about that baby and he finds out... I mean, wouldn't that be pretty shitty? That's his baby in there."

"I know. But..."

"Babies don't ruin lives, Bronwyn. They make them better. At least from what I've seen. People make it work. Dylan will make it work. I don't think he'll resent you, or the baby. What he will resent, is if you don't even give him the fucking option."

I jerked my head back and held up my hands. "Whoa, Lisa. I didn't say anything about swearing at your boss."

"Sorry," she whispered.

"I'm kidding." I couldn't help myself, I reached out and hugged her. "I needed that. I needed someone to stand up to me and tell me that I was being a jerk."

"Not a jerk." Lisa pulled away from the hug. "You're just a crazy pregnant lady."

"A crazy pregnant lady who needs another one of these. Maybe you can show me how to do it?" I asked.

"Sure." Lisa handed me the glasses. "You can start by rinsing these."

For the rest of the morning, Lisa and I worked together around the bunkie. I did things I've never done in my entire life – like work the washing machine. Lisa told me that I'd be doing laundry every day with the baby.

While I was getting my crash course in keeping a house, I kept an eye on the time. Was Dylan going to call me about the fishing date, or was I supposed to call him? I couldn't remember. By the time Lisa and I were preparing a salad for lunch I was exhausted.

"Lisa. I think I need a nap." I set down the peeler and took a bite of a half-peeled carrot.

She laughed. "You're going to have to work on your stamina, but I think you and Dylan and baby Moss are going to be just fine."

I gave her a thankful smile and retreated to my bedroom where I pulled out a notebook and started to compose a letter to my family. The letter I would hand to them after I told Dylan about the baby. Even though my mind was racing, my tired body won the fight and I fell asleep imagining how I would paint one of the bedrooms at Dylan's house for the nursery. Everything was going to be okay. I didn't need my family or their money. All I needed was Dylan, and as soon as I saw him again, I was going to tell him everything.

TWENTY
DYLAN

EVEN THOUGH THE days were getting shorter, and the tops of the maple trees were starting to show the first signs of fall, it was one of the hottest days of the summer. I pulled the bandana from the back pocket of my pants and wiped my forehead.

The smell of grease hung heavy in the air, and I didn't think I could eat, but the rest of the mechanics had gone for the special fish and chips at the food truck. I joined the crew, taking a seat at one of the picnic tables sheltered by a striped umbrella. I was able to get down a French fry but just poked at the chunk of battered pickerel. My stomach had been in knots since the morning visit from Mr. Yates.

While the crew talked about engines and their families, my mind kept replaying the events of the morning, wishing it had gone differently. I had lost the sale of my boat and the approval of Bronwyn's father. I hadn't just lost his approval; I was pretty sure he downright hated me. There was always a divide between the Laketownies and the cottagers, but I had never witnessed it firsthand and never as harshly as that morning.

"Moss." Luke, one of the junior mechanics snapped his fingers in front of my face. "Whatcha thinking about?" He had a huge grin on his face.

As the crew came into focus, I realized that they were all staring at me and each of them was wearing a shit-eating grin.

"What?" I asked.

Luke held out his phone. "Looks like you've got yourself a new girlfriend."

The image on the phone was a little blurry, but it was clear enough to see that a beautiful blond woman was wrapped in my arms – the number on my Otters' jacket was in the foreground. There was no denying that it was me in the photo.

I shrugged. "No big deal."

"It's in the *York Tattler*." Luke thrust the phone in my face again, like I hadn't seen the image the first time. "Your little girlfriend is a billionaire."

"And the hottest chick on the lake." Mark, another mechanic chimed in.

"Come on, Mossy. Spill." Luke elbowed me.

I could feel the blood rushing to my face. One of the mechanics was going to get an old-school hockey beatdown if they kept talking about Bronwyn like that. "She's my friend." At least that part was true. The girlfriend part? After the confrontation with Peter Yates, I didn't know anymore.

"Sure. Sure." Mark took a swig of his coffee and shoved a piece of fish into his mouth. "Friends who fuck." He laughed.

The other guys didn't join in and avoided looking at me. I could feel my nostrils flaring and my hands were balled into fists under the picnic table. After a terrible morning, I couldn't take any of this bullshit.

But instead of hopping over the table and punching Mark in the face, I dabbed my mouth with the paper napkin and closed my take-out container. "I'm going back to work," I growled.

"Sorry, Moss," Mark whispered. "Come on, you know I was joking – but seriously, the ass on that woman…"

I dropped my food and slapped both hands on the table. I leaned across the table, so I was within head-butting distance of Mark. "You're lucky I have a game tomorrow night, otherwise this fist would be through your face right now."

Mark gave himself a double chin as he tried to get his face as far away from mine as possible. He held his hands up in front of him. "Take it easy, Moss."

"Not good enough," I seethed.

"Sorry," he muttered under his breath.

"For what?" I was still seething.

"For insulting your…"

"Bronwyn." I finished his sentence. "I'm sorry for insulting Bronwyn."

"I'm sorry for insulting Bronwyn." He stared at the table as he spoke.

"That's better." I picked up my lunch and threw it in the trash as I headed back to the marina. Even if Mr. Yates wasn't going to buy my boat project, someone else would – and I needed to get it done. The bays of the marina were sweltering hot, and I slipped into Floyd's office to get a glass of water before I started sanding Bronwyn's fingerprint from the varnish.

I was so focused on the task that I hadn't noticed that someone was behind me until I felt the tap on my shoulder.

"Looks good, Kid." Floyd crossed his arms across his chest and leaned to inspect my work. "How did it go this morning?"

I sighed and blew away the sanding dust. "Not great."

"Floyd?" Thelma's voice echoed through the shop, interrupting our conversation.

"Over here, sweetie," he shouted. "Just talking to Dylan."

"Oh, good. Tell him line two is for him."

Floyd patted me on the shoulder. "Better luck with the next one. You heard the woman – line two."

Thankful for the interruption, I picked up the shop phone and pressed the flashing line two button. "Dylan Moss," I said as the line connected.

"Dylan Moss." It was a woman's voice on the other end of the line, but one that I didn't recognize.

"Can I help you?" It was pretty rare for me to speak directly to a customer; the calls typically went through the service desk.

The cackle on the other end of the phone was so loud I had to hold the receiver away from my ear. "You think you're good enough to be with my daughter?"

I felt like the floor had turned into quicksand and I leaned against the wall to get my balance. "Mrs. Yates?"

The evil laugh rang through the phone again. "Who else would it be? One of the other rich girls' mommies?"

I held the received out from my ear and looked at it, wondering if I could just hang up.

"What do you want?" I asked quietly.

"What do you s-s-shink I want?" Her voice was slurred, and I wondered if she was drunk. I glanced at my watch, and it wasn't even noon, and I was seriously running low on patience. "Mrs. Yates, is there something I can do for you?" I was trying to keep calm. First Mr. Yates, then Mark, and now Mrs. Yates.

"Yes!" she yelled into the phone. "Go find another rich girl. You'll never weasel your way into our fortune."

"Weasel?" I spoke through clenched teeth. "Mrs. Yates, I love your daughter. I don't care about the money."

Her laugh sounded almost maniacal. "Bull. Shit. A little

Laketownie like you? You all dream of sinking your dirty little fingernails into a girl like Bronwyn."

"Mrs. Yates, it sounds like you've had a little too much to drink."

"Don't you tell me what to do. Mr. Yates and I have decided that you need to go away."

"Excuse me?" The Yates were a powerful family. "Is that a threat?"

"Of course not." Her voice had taken on a sinister tone. "I will wire fifty thousand dollars to your bank account if you promise to never talk to Bronwyn ever again."

I knew that I had to get off the phone, but I couldn't let her get away with speaking to me like I was a second-class citizen. "I love your daughter and she loves me. I don't need your approval, but I will prove to you that I only have good intentions. And I will not stay away from Bronwyn." I wasn't going to let this drunk rich lady keep me from the woman that I loved.

The line was silent. "You don't know." Her voice was low.

"I don't know what?" If I didn't love Bronwyn the way I did, my potential mother-in-law being a deranged lunatic would've been enough to send me packing.

"About the baby."

"What baby—"

She laughed even louder. "Oh, honey. Didn't you notice your precious girlfriend was getting a little fat?"

I didn't know what to say and there were at least two full seconds of silence before Mrs. Yates laughed again. "Oh, you poor little thing. Your perfect girl isn't so perfect after all. Ask yourself how you could love someone who keeps a secret like that from you."

"Fuck. You. And fuck your fifty thousand dollars." I hung up the phone.

This couldn't be happening to me.

TWENTY-ONE
BRONWYN

THE CURTAINS WERE BLOWING in the wind when I woke up from my nap. I groaned as I pushed myself into a sitting position and stretched my hands over my head. Something felt weird on my back, and I contorted my arm to reach behind me and felt the paper from the letter I had started to write to my parents. I peeled it off my sweaty skin and squinted out the window. The sun was shining brightly, and the lake sparkled in the distance.

"Lisa?" I walked to the air conditioner thermostat and tapped it. "Is this thing working?"

Lisa appeared beside me; a tea towel draped over her shoulder. I just turned the temperature down, it's a scorcher out there today."

"How long was I sleeping?"

"About four hours," Lisa yelled as she returned to the kitchen. "You missed lunch."

My stomach growled and I followed her to the kitchen. "Is the salad still good?"

She laughed. "It is. I didn't put the dressing on it yet." Lisa took the salad from the refrigerator and sliced a barbecued chicken breast to put on top.

"Thank you." I dug in. "I can't believe I slept for so long."

Lisa pointed to my belly. "You are making a human in there."

"I suppose that takes some energy, doesn't it?" I crunched a fork full of greens into my mouth.

Lisa sat on the barstool beside me. "Bronwyn, have you done any research into this pregnancy? What kind of birth do you want to have? Are you taking the right vitamins?"

I set down the fork and smoothed the linen napkin on my lap. "I was going to buy a book online. I just kind of, I don't know Lisa. This isn't how I wanted things to go."

"If everyone waited until they were ready, nobody would have a baby." She took her phone out of her pocket and typed something into the browser. "At least, that's the quote that makes everyone feel better about it." She turned the phone toward me so I could see the bookstore app and a pregnancy book. "This is your first present. I'll get it sent to my house."

"You don't have to do that, Lisa."

Lisa pushed at the screen of her phone and then set it down. "Already done."

My phone chimed and I picked it up. "It's a message from Dylan." I couldn't stop the smile from spreading across my face.

"Oh," I whispered as I read the message.

"What is it?" Lisa asked.

Disappointment flooded my body. "He can't go fishing tonight. He's busy."

"Good. You need some rest." Lisa patted my leg. "Don't read into it, Bronwyn. He's probably…" she paused. "Busy."

"You're right." I put the phone down, but there was a sinking feeling in my stomach that I couldn't explain. My intuition was telling me that something was wrong. "I'm heading out for a little bit."

Lisa raised her eyebrows at me.

"Don't worry, I'm not doing something stupid." I shoved my phone into my purse and grabbed a tube of lipstick from the bathroom. Dylan was off work at five. I could catch him right when he was done and tell him about the baby. It felt urgent. I couldn't keep the secret for one more second.

My grandmother's dockhand was polishing *Calliope* and waved at me as I rushed into the boathouse. "Hi, Eddie," I shouted over the sound of the waves lapping in the boathouse.

"Good afternoon, Miss Yates." Eddie paused his polishing to stand. "Do you need me to get your boat ready?"

I glanced at my runabout, it was sitting in the lift, but the Boston Whaler was floating in the water beside her. "I'll take the Whaler." I pointed to the boat that was ready to go.

"Are you sure, Miss? It will only take a couple of minutes to get yours ready." He had walked to the lift beside my royal blue boat.

"No, I'm in a rush, Eddie. I have to go now." My voice was a lot more panicky than I'd expected.

"Of course, Miss Yates." Eddie took the keys for the Whaler from the safe by the door and handed them to me. "I'll get the lines."

"Thank you, Eddie." I hopped into the boat and my heart soared when she started right away. The Whaler was a plain white boat with no bells and whistles, but she was sturdy and fast – exactly what I needed. I reversed out of the boathouse and when I was clear of the docks, I pushed down the throttle. My hair whipped my cheeks as I ran the Whaler at top speed down the middle of Lake Casper. Luckily, it was a calm day and there wasn't much boat traffic and I pulled into the marina at five minutes to five.

"Hello, Miss Yates." Sam tied the lines and helped me from the boat.

"Fill her up please, Sam."

The young man nodded. I didn't know if the boat needed gas, it was highly unlikely as Eddie kept the fleet topped up with fuel at all times, but it was a good excuse to be at the marina. "I'll be in the shop." I smiled at Sam and rushed to the big blue building, knowing that my life was about to change.

TWENTY-TWO

DYLAN

I⊤ WAS SO humid that the first coat of varnish hadn't dried. "Dammit," I whispered under my breath. I was hoping to get the second coat on that evening.

The atmosphere in the garage that afternoon had been strained. Mike and Luke avoided me, and so did the rest of the guys. It suited me just fine, I needed to get work done, and I didn't want to talk to anyone – so I stewed. As it got hotter, as the sun rose higher in the sky, baking the metal building, I stewed even harder.

The phone call from Mrs. Yates had weighed heavily on me like I had been wearing lead shoulder pads all day long. Could it be true? Was Bronwyn pregnant? Is that why she didn't want to sleep with me? Could the baby be mine? As the marina heated up with the afternoon sun, my mind had gone to darker places. Was she trying to pin this baby on me? That didn't make sense, but nothing else made sense either.

Floyd and Thelma were holding hands as they left for the day. "See you, Dylan." Floyd waved.

"Bye," I shouted. I would've made a joke about white-haired love birds, but I didn't feel like joking.

With everyone gone, I plugged my phone into the sound system and turned on some Metallica. I needed something loud and angry. I knew that avoiding Bronwyn wasn't the mature thing to do, I should've marched over to the Yates Estate and demanded to know the truth – but I had to calm down first. I had to get my mind straight before I did that. I planned to work on the boat and then get Andy to let me into the rink. The best therapy was puck therapy – and nothing got frustration out of a body like cold air, skating fast, and slap shots.

The bell to the store rang and I groaned. Typical. Some entitled cottager coming in just as we were closing. Probably to get ice for martinis or some shit like that. I would let Sam deal with it.

I rolled under the boat on a dolly and ran the sandpaper along any sections that didn't look absolutely perfect. As I took out my anger sanding, a pair of manicured toes in expensive-looking sandals approached.

"We're closed," I grumbled as loud as I could.

The pedicured foot nudged my work boot. I slid out from under the boat and my angry heart softened a little when my eyes met hers.

"Sam is filling up the boat. I thought I would come in and say hi." She reached her hand to help me up from my position on the dolly.

"Hi." I ignored her hand and rolled back under the boat.

She stood there for what felt like a minute but was probably about ten seconds. "I guess I'll go then." She turned and started to walk away.

I took a deep breath and pushed out from under the boat hard enough that the wheeled dolly caught up with her. "Sorry. Long day." I hopped up and kicked the dolly towards the boat.

Bronwyn reached to hug me, but I pushed her back by

her hips. "I'm all sweaty." It was the truth, I was covered in sweat, sawdust, and oil – but that wasn't the reason I didn't want to hug her.

"I don't care." She smiled and reached her arms for me.

I took a step back. "I do care." I walked back to the boat. "I'm trying to get this done tonight. Thanks for the visit." I didn't want to meet her eyes.

"Dylan."

I had to look at her. She was stunning.

"Could you turn down the music a little?" she shouted and pointed to the speaker.

I turned it off completely and then it was just the two of us in the silence. I rubbed the dry section of the boat with a chamois and tried to keep my hands busy. All I wanted to do was scoop her up in my arms, to feel her lips on mine – but she had lied to me.

"Is everything okay with us?" She came around the boat, so she was standing directly next to me.

I kept polishing. "I don't know. Is it?"

"Why are you being an asshole?" Her voice was lower.

She was the fourth person to confront me that day, and I guess I was at the end of my rope. "An asshole?" I growled. "I could ask you the same question."

"What?" She took a step away from me.

"Yeah." I crossed my arms across my chest. "You know, Bronwyn, there are a lot of rumors about you and your family – and…" I hacked out a laugh. "I defended you. You might be a lot of things, Bron. But I didn't think that you were a liar."

Her bottom lip started to quiver. "A liar? Dylan, what are you talking about?"

"Are you, or are you not pregnant?"

Her face went white. "Dylan." Her eyes filled with tears, and she reached for my hand. "I meant to tell you."

"It's true then. Why didn't you tell me? You were just going to have fun with your little white trash boyfriend? Is this why it was a big secret?" The pieces started to fall into place and my voice got louder. "You weren't protecting me, were you, Bron? This wasn't about hiding me and my background from the paparazzi. It was about protecting you."

The anger that had been simmering all day boiled over. I shook my head and couldn't look at her. "After everything we've been through, you hid something from me."

She kicked at the concrete floor with the toe of her sandal. "I had to wait for the right time, Dylan."

"The right time," I scoffed. "If you weren't using me, you would've told me."

Tears were streaming down her face, and I hated the fact that I was yelling, but I couldn't stop myself. "Whose is it, Bron? Mine? One of your other boy toys?" Just the idea of it made me want to punch a hole in a wall. "If it were mine, you would've told me," I added. "It wouldn't make sense to keep that secret from the father." Over Bronwyn's shoulder, I could see my reflection in the mirror and my face was as red as a navigational marker.

She swiped at the tears on her face and stormed to the door. "You're a lot of things too, Dylan." She shook her finger at me. "But I didn't think that you were a complete and utter asshole." A gust of wind blew her hair as she opened the door. "And don't worry. The baby isn't yours."

TWENTY-THREE
DYLAN

THE NEXT NIGHT, Coach walked into the dressing room, and we collectively held our breath. I knew Coach better than most guys on the team and I could usually read him like a playbook, but after tying up game two in the series, I couldn't tell what he was feeling.

Coach Covington whispered something to Leo who nodded and started drawing up a play on the whiteboard.

"Come in close, guys." Coach waved for us to meet him in the center of the room.

I looked at Mike and he wrinkled his brow at me. We both shrugged and joined the rest of the team in a huddle around our coach.

"That was a great two periods." Coach was speaking so quietly that we all had to take a step in to hear him.

"Mike, great assist. Jasper, perfect slapshot…" As Coach praised all the guys who had scored or done something decent in the first two periods, I kind of zoned out. Usually, intense emotion made me play better, but since I found out about Bronwyn's deception, I couldn't channel all that anger into a goal. The intense sexual buildup that had fueled my strides… hell, it was gone.

"Moss," Coach shouted, and I snapped my eyes to him. "Did I interrupt your little daydream? Were you imagining scoring a goal? Were you imagining actually completing a play?"

"Sorry, Coach." I was blowing it.

The rest of the pep talk went by in a blur and the team seemed pumped to get out and play, but my heart wasn't in it.

And I wasn't the only one who could tell. Jasper was playing like there were National League scouts in the box seats because there were. He scored the winning goal with one minute to spare. My feet were cold inside my skates and had practically fallen asleep. Coach had benched me for the entire last period, and I didn't feel like celebrating.

"Come on, Moss." Mike slapped my back as he hopped over the boards. I followed him and joined the rest of the guys at center ice as they celebrated the win. After shaking hands with the disgraced National League team, I followed my team to the dressing room.

"Hey, Mike." I grabbed the sleeve of his jersey before we went into the dressing room. "Do you mind making the team speech?" As captain, I usually said a few words after each game, but as the assistant, Mike could do it too.

"Sure, Captain." Mike pressed his lips into a line and nodded, but before he went in, he turned to me. "What happened to you out there?"

I sighed. "I don't know. My head's not in the right place."

"Dylan." He grabbed the back of my head so hard it made me wince. "Get your fucking head in the game." And he turned and pulled the door open so hard it banged against the concrete wall.

❄

THE BREW PUB was standing room only. Fans were lined down the sidewalk hoping for a chance to mingle with the Otters and some of the National League guys. A pitcher of beer sat in the middle of the table and my mouth was salivating.

I hadn't officially quit drinking, I just hadn't drunk in a long time and I was pretty sure that I could have just one. As I poured a glass of beer from the pitcher, I caught Leo watching me. He narrowed his lips but returned to the conversation beside him. Sweat beaded on the outside of the glass and I sat mesmerized, watching the bubbles rise from the bottom.

"Dylan." Leo slid into the chair beside me.

I groaned. "Hi, drink police. It's just one."

"I know, buddy." He smiled. "But I have a better offer for you."

"Oh, yeah?" I chuckled. "What's that?"

"Come with me." Leo slid the beer away from me. My instinct was to reach for the glass and slam the hoppy beverage down as fast as I could – that's when I knew that it wouldn't have been 'just one.' But what did it matter? I looked at my friend and assistant coach and then at the glass of beer. I could be just like all the other guys in town. I could play beer league hockey with all the guys. I could grow old and gray and out of shape and drink a twelve-pack every night after work. It would be easy. Hell, it's what was expected of me.

Leo put his hand on my shoulder. "I know what you're thinking."

I laughed and turned to look up at him. "I highly doubt that."

"You're feeling sorry for yourself and planning to become

another town drunk."

The bubbles had stopped rising to the top of the beer and my mouth was watering for it. "So, what if I am?"

"You're more than that."

"Maybe I'm not."

Leo narrowed his eyes at me. "Get the fuck out of that chair and stop feeling sorry for yourself."

"Are you asking me or telling me?" Leo was lucky that I wasn't ten beers in. My hands were balled into fists at my side and drunk me would've punched that self-righteous prick in the nose.

Leo hadn't moved his hand from my shoulder, and he squeezed it, a little tighter than a friendly squeeze. "I'm asking you – as a friend. And as your coach. It's important."

His patience and kindness won me over. He didn't want to see me spiral out of control, even though that's all I felt like doing. It was the easiest way to get over Bronwyn.

"Alright." I handed the beer to Jasper and followed Leo from the Brewpub.

"Where are we going?"

Leo pointed to my car. "Get your hockey bag and come with me."

I sighed and pulled the big Bauer bag from the trunk and threw it in the back of his rusty old pickup truck. "I would've been fine. There's just a lot going on."

The gears ground as Leo put the truck in gear and I wound down the window and let the breeze blow through the cab as we drove through town. "A lot more than being shortlisted for the New York Thunder?" Leo glanced at me and then returned his gaze to the road.

"What?"

Leo grinned. "Yep. They're interested in you, even after you shit the bed in tonight's game."

"How do you know?" I turned down the radio so I could

focus on his every word. My life had been turned upside down and this was the first piece of good news I'd had in two days.

"If I told you, I'd have to kill you." The truck shocks creaked as we pulled into McManus Place.

"What are we doing here?" I asked.

"You're getting your mojo back." Leo turned off the engine but didn't get out of the car. "We're going to go work on your slapshot. It's the best in the league, everyone knows that. You lost it tonight. We're not leaving the ice until you get it back."

I groaned. "I haven't lost it, Lion. I just had a tough couple of days."

"Maybe you should start by telling me about it and then we're going to get some ice therapy."

The tears welled up and I swiped at my face, hoping that Leo hadn't seen. "Thanks, Leo."

"For what?" He jiggled the keys to get them from the ignition.

My voice croaked, "Being my friend."

Leo paused with his hand on the truck door and looked like he might cry too. He took a visibly deep breath. "I know you'd do the same thing for me."

I totally would. I put the other guys' goals, hopes, and aspirations ahead of my own – maybe it was time to start treating myself as the MVP. "I was seeing Bronwyn Yates. In secret."

Leo smiled and his eyes glinted. "I don't think it was that 'secret'. Your photo was in the Tattler."

I inhaled deeply. "She finally decided that we could be seen together and then…"

The interior light slowly faded, and we sat in the cab in darkness.

"And then…" he urged.

"It all fell apart. Part of me thought that if I could make it to the National League, I would finally be worthy of her. That I could be accepted into her world. It turns out she's just a liar and was using me."

"Fuck," Leo whispered under his breath. "Really? That's cold. She seemed so genuine and into you at the pizza party."

The Rolls Royce night. The kissing in the rain night, the most amazing blowjob in the back of the car night. I could feel the anger creeping through my body. How could I have been so blind? No wonder she didn't want me to drop her off at her cottage. I was just her dirty little secret.

"Come on." I hopped out of the car. "I'm ready to smash the shit out of some biscuits."

With the interior light on, I could see the smile on Leo's face. "That's what I'm talking about." He grabbed his bag of equipment. "Andy is going to join us."

"Really? That's awesome." Back in the day, Andy, the Zamboni driver was one of the top players in the Northern Professional League.

The moon shone brightly as I walked into my second home – the rink, alongside my best friend. I didn't need Bronwyn, and I didn't need that beer either. I wasn't going to make it to the National League for Bronwyn. I was going to make it for my own fucking self.

TWENTY-FOUR
BRONWYN

THE RAIN PINGED off the metal roof of the bunkie and I rolled over in bed, not ready or wanting to face Lisa. She had arrived an hour earlier and had been busying herself in the kitchen, waiting for me to get up to hand me a smoothie. I pulled the covers over my head, and I felt like I drifted off to sleep on and off for days.

A soft knock on the door woke me up from my half-sleep. "Miss Bronwyn, are you alright?" Lisa opened the door a crack.

"I'm okay," I grumbled from under the nest of blankets. "I'm going to get up – in a little bit."

Lisa shut the door and then opened it again. "Miss Bronwyn, it's past noon."

I sat up and hoped that my face wasn't as puffy looking as it felt. I had cried myself to sleep the night before. "Okay. I'll get up."

"Zeesh. Your face. What happened?" She crossed her arms and took a few steps into my bedroom. There was a book tucked under her arm.

"What's that?" I pointed to the book.

"It's the pregnancy book I was telling you about. I thought that you might want to learn about what's going on in your body." Lisa did something unprecedented and sat on the edge of my bed. "What happened?" she whispered.

I propped myself up on the down pillows and as I spoke, I wound my hair into a loose braid. "I messed everything up."

"With Dylan?" Her eyes shone with concern.

"Yeah." I nodded. "With Dylan. But it's probably a good thing. He said some cruel things and was a total asshole."

"Do you want to talk about it?" Lisa set the book on the nightstand. "I can bring your smoothie in here."

"No." I swung my legs out of the bed. "It's time for me to take control of my life. To figure out what the hell I'm doing, and to put this little guy first." I rubbed my belly. "This might not be the only time my family held my inheritance over my head, but I needed to become self-sufficient – and through my wallowing, had come up with a business idea.

"It's a boy?" Lisa couldn't seem to stop the grin from spreading across her face.

I stood and stretched my arms over my head and caught a glimpse of myself in the mirror. The long braid tumbled over her shoulder. My eyes were rimmed red and my face puffier than after a night of too much Dom Perignon. "I don't know for sure. I just kind of... know."

Lisa backed to the door. "Women's intuition. I believe in that."

I thought that I believed in it too. But I had been wrong about Dylan. "For some things, I think we get it right. I rubbed my lower back, which had been getting tighter and tighter every day. I'll come and have the smoothie and then do you want to go to a yoga class together?"

Lisa raised her eyebrows. "A yoga class?"

"It will be on the clock."

Lisa looked me up and down as if assessing my mental

health. "Sure, Miss Bronwyn. I'd love to go to a yoga class with you."

"But first, smoothie" I smiled and followed Lisa into the kitchen, and over a gritty spirulina and kale smoothie, spilled my guts to my cleaning lady. The whole thing.

"I still can't believe you told him it wasn't his." Lisa's tone was quiet, but there was a sternness to it – subtle disapproval that I tried to ignore.

I sighed and sucked through the metal straw. "I did him a favor. It turns out he's an asshole. I set him free."

Lisa's lips narrowed, but instead of saying anything, she finished her smoothie with a slurp.

"Do you think that was a mistake?" I didn't want to hear the answer.

Lisa rinsed her cup in the sink and her shoulders slumped before she turned to face me. "It's not for me to say."

She didn't have to say it out loud, and I knew it too. Lying to Dylan the first time had been wrong – lying to him the second time had been one of the worst things I'd ever done in my life.

"I've royally fucked everything up," I cried. "But I can't go back now." I pushed the half-gone smoothie away. "I'm not hungry."

"What about yoga?" Lisa asked.

I slipped off the barstool. "I'm tired. I'm going to go back to bed."

Her eyes followed me with concern. I turned and shook my finger at her. "Don't you judge me."

"Never, Miss Bronwyn," Lisa said. "You're one of the best people I've ever met. Even the best people make mistakes."

I almost cried again, but there just weren't any more tears left in my body. "I-I just need some sleep." I went back to my sea of white sheets and collapsed back into bed.

Two days later, I was wearing the same nightgown and had been living off of Lisa's smoothies. "You're getting out of bed today." Lisa had gotten bolder and stormed into my room and pulled the duvet off the bed. I curled into a fetal position. "Noooo. I just want to stay here and…"

"Wallow?" Lisa finished my sentence.

"Yeah. Wallow."

"I can't let you do that." Lisa set a glass of water on the nightstand.

"Please." I tried to grab the duvet from the floor, but Lisa snatched it away.

With the bundle of covers in her arms, Lisa stared me down. "I've let you sleep away the last two and a half days. It's time for you to get up and think about your next move. You mentioned a business idea – do that. You're not the kind of woman to play the victim. And…" she paused.

"And what?" I eyed her up. I didn't like her tone.

"And your mom is here today. And your grandmother…"

"Ugh." I rolled my eyes. "Grandma Yates is here?" The woman was never seen in anything less than a perfect outfit. She ran the company until she was in her fifties, and even after retiring kept a position on the board of directors. She was a tough lady who definitely wouldn't spend two days in bed feeling sorry for herself.

"Yep. Time to pull yourself together. I think that you're starting to get a rat's nest in that Rapunzel braid of yours."

Reaching to the braid confirmed the rat's nest comment. Lisa was right. What was done was done. It was time for me to get dressed and put on some lipstick – but first a shower.

As I wiped the steam from the mirror, I replayed the conversation with Dylan over and over again. Of course, he was upset. A bombshell had just been dropped on him. I still hadn't figured out who had told him. There were very few people who knew about the pregnancy, and I couldn't imagine any one of them telling Dylan. I had to explain everything to him. If he knew what was truly going on, he might not hate me. If the whole story came out in the open, would he still want to be with me? A love like we have doesn't just die like that, does it?

I had to figure out how to reach him and have a real conversation together. I had been immature – and so had he. It was time to grow up.

TWENTY-FIVE
DYLAN

SCALPERS LINED the streets of Laketown hours before the final game in the exhibition series. Cars drove up and down the main street trailing Otters flags and blue and white jerseys dotted the sidewalks – even in the warmth of the summer.

It felt like a lightning bolt had hit Laketown and the energy from the strike had hung around, infecting every fan in town. I rolled my wrists as I drove to the rink, they were a little sore from the slapshot session the other night with Leo and Andy. For an old dude, I think he's in his late thirties, Andy could play. The three of us skated until the ice was so carved up from our blades it felt like an old bumpy pond. With the pressure off, the love for the game shone through and I left McManus Place feeling a little more hopeful. With each shot, I focused more on my career and less on the blue eyes of Bronwyn Yates.

Don't get me wrong. It still hurt like hell, but if there's anything to help get me over heartache – it's hockey.

I still couldn't help myself from scanning the audience as we warmed up. The bass from the music was vibrating the walls of the stadium and the crowd was on their feet. Jessie and Kane were sitting in a private box and even though I knew it was unrealistic, part of me hoped to see a certain blond sitting in there with them.

As the thought hit me, I wound up and the crowd cheered as my slapshot practically ripped through the back of the net. I had to forget about Bronwyn and focus on the game. This was my night. I could feel it.

Both teams scored in the first period. We were aggressive and our offensive lines dominated the first fifteen minutes. In the second period, the experience of the pros left us chasing the puck more than we would have liked, but our defense held steady. After the second period, the score was still tied one to one.

Coach was uncharacteristically cool in the dressing room between periods. Usually, a garbage can got kicked over and his level of profanity would make any trucker blush. We had started the game strong but were fading – everyone could feel it.

"Moss." Coach pointed at me with his pen. "Your favorite goal of the year – what was it?"

I smiled. "Easy. The first goal I scored in this series."

"Good answer!" Coach laughed. "Everyone, shut your eyes and imagine the puck on your stick. Imagine the sound of the audience screaming."

We all looked at each other before the majority of the guys shrugged and followed along with Coach's weird Zen visualization exercise.

Coach's voice sounded lower and had a little more gravel to it. With my eyes shut I could see the puck on my stick, I could hear the audience.

"Now…" Coach's voice was getting louder. "Imagine the sound of your name being announced through the speakers." I could hear it – I swore I could. The same announcer had worked at the arena since I was a kid, and I could hear his voice in my sleep some nights. I could see the puck as I wrapped around the net and backhanded it through the five-hole. The shock in the goalie's eyes when he realized that the puck was behind him – and I could see the glow of the goal light flashing. The faces of my teammates as they congratulated me were clear as day. The face in the audience screaming and clapping my name came into my visualization before I could stop it. I squeezed my eyes hard to try to get Bronwyn out of the picture.

"Open your eyes," Coach yelled.

The room came into fuzzy view as I blinked my eyes open. I could feel the adrenaline surging through my body.

Coach looked at all of us and then whispered so we all had to lean in. "Could you see it?"

Most of the guys nodded and a few of them grumbled a yes.

"No," Coach's voice was louder and then he yelled, the baritone of his voice echoing in the room. "Could you fucking see it?"

The room erupted as all the players launched to their feet and roared.

Leo and Coach smiled as they surveyed the frenzied energy in the dressing room. We weren't Otters, we were sharks and the coach had just thrown some chum in the water.

Coach opened the door. "Now get out there and play some hockey."

The cheering got louder and we all high-fived Coach and Leo as we headed to the ice for the most important period of hockey in our career.

Through experience, I knew that the first minute of the third period would set the tone. As I reached center ice, the sounds of McManus Place disappeared to a buzz. The audience turned into a sea blue of white, and all I could see and hear was the action on the ice. I met the eyes of the Jaguar's captain at the faceoff and made him look away first. As the puck dropped, it seemed to move in slow motion. I picked it away from the Jaguar and within two strides passed it to Jasper, my right-winger, and then flew up the center of the ice. I never thought about skating, it just happened, my legs seemed to have a mind of their own and I didn't even worry about what they were doing – because they were doing it fast and they were doing it well.

Jasper passed the puck to Mike who faked the shot, which gave me just enough time to reach the side of the net. Just as in my visualization, I rounded the net with the puck on the heel of my stick and before the goalie knew what had happened, I had slipped the puck in between the goalie's pads. The light flashed and it was as though my visualization had completely come to life – the crowded team hug – and the glance to the private box. And that's where it ended. Kane and Jessie were hopping up and down, waving their arms and screaming. The seat beside them – well, it was as I knew it would be – empty.

We held the two to one lead until the last minute of play when one of their players got a slap shot past our goalie. If we could have only held out one minute longer, we would have won the game.

Even with the goalie pulled for the last minute of play and an extra Otter on the ice, we didn't have it in us to even out the score – and the big star of the Jaguars lobbed a shot, and a second before the buzzer sounded, it slid into our net.

When the game clock sounded, the Jaguars had beaten the Otters three to two.

We were the underdogs, and for a while, I thought the Otters were going to have a Cinderella story. Most of the guys went out to celebrate anyway, but all I wanted to do was shower and go home. The past few days had taken their toll on me, and I just wanted to be alone.

After an hour of signing autographs after the game, I got in my old beat-up car and drove home in silence.

THE TV WAS FLICKING in the darkened room when a knock on the door woke me from a dreamless sleep, propped up on the old sofa in the living room. The remote control clattered to the floor as I sat up and tried to turn on some lights.

Bang, bang, bang.

"Jesus, hold on." Whoever it was, they knocked like a cop.

Even though part of me hoped it was Bronwyn, I knew that she'd never want to see me again after how I spoke to her. I was a total dick, but I mean, come on – I don't know any dude who wouldn't react like that after finding out the woman he was in love with was carrying another man's baby.

After turning on the porch light, I saw that the muscle behind the knock was Jessie, and I opened the door.

"Are you locking this now?" she joked. Growing up we had never locked the front door, and usually, Jessie would just walk in whenever she felt like it. Technically she still lived there – her room was still set up with all of her figure skater posters and teddy bears covered in medals.

"New habit." I didn't remember locking the door, but there was something about being threatened by a billionaire that made me a little more cautious.

"Great game." Jessie gave me a huge hug.

"Thanks. I mean, I guess." I looked behind Jessie, but there was no sign of her fiancé. "Where's Kane?"

"He went to go party with some of the Jaguars."

"Right. The winning team."

"You stop that." Jessie walked past me and settled into the recliner in the living room. "What are you watching?"

"Did you come to check on me?" Jessie and I weren't really in the habit of watching TV together anymore.

Jessie pulled the handle to fully recline the chair. "Not like that. I mean, I just wanted to talk to you about the game. I knew you'd be beating yourself up about losing. Even if you scored the most beautiful goal I've ever seen and that everyone in town will be talking about for years."

I couldn't help but smile. "It was pretty good, wasn't it? He thought I was going to go high, and I went low."

"I thought you were going to go high too!" Jessie clapped her hands together. I couldn't believe it. Dyl…" Her voice got serious.

"Yeah?" Something told me I wasn't going to like the next part of the conversation.

"Why aren't you out with your team? Is it hard to celebrate without drinking?"

I took a deep breath. "I should be out with them, and no, it's not all that hard to go out without drinking. I've been doing it for a while now."

"I've noticed," she beamed.

"It's just, I've had a rough couple of days." I reclined onto the couch in my usual spot and fluffed the pillow behind my head.

"I-I-I noticed that Bronwyn wasn't at the game tonight," she stammered, which she never does. She knew that she was entering sticky territory. I was glad that all of the living room furniture pointed at the television, so we didn't have to have any awkward eye contact.

"Nope."

My reaction would've stopped a normal person from continuing with the conversation, but my sister was relentless. "What's going on with you guys?"

I flicked through a few channels before I answered. "Nothing,"

"Is that nothing why you haven't been yourself for the past few days? Or, why you played like shit at the last game?"

"Hey." I sat up and looked at her. "It wasn't our worst game ever."

Jessie rolled her eyes. "I suppose that's true. I've seen you guys shit the bed worse than that before. But don't deke the question, mister. What happened with that girl?"

I shut my eyes and tried to figure out how much of the story to tell my sister. "I don't want to talk about it."

Jessie released the footrest of the recliner and came over to sit beside me. "That's why you should. You know that not talking about Mom and Dad was bad for both of us. We had to learn the hard way that bottling up feelings is not good for the Moss kids."

She had a point.

"And I saw you two together. When she talked about you Dylan, that woman lit up."

I saw it too, but now I knew better – she wasn't radiant because of our relationship, she was glowing because she was pregnant. "She did something I can't forgive."

Jessie breathed in sharply. "She cheated on you?"

"Well, no." Technically she hadn't – that I knew of.

"Then what could she have done that you can't forgive?" Jessie tucked one foot up underneath her and kept her gaze trained on me. There was no point in lying to her – she could tell if I was hiding something – the same way I could tell if she was doing it to me.

Deep breaths were going to get me through the conversation, and I took a very drawn-out inhale and exhale. "She wanted to have this 'secret' relationship." I used air quotes around *secret*. "But it was because she was embarrassed by me."

"That doesn't make any sense. She was all over you after the game – in front of the entire town." Jessie's brow was furrowed.

"Yeah, well. We decided that we weren't going to be a 'secret' anymore. Then, I asked her dad for permission to date her, and he told me to stay away from her."

"Ouch," Jessie grimaced.

"Oh," I laughed. "That's not the worst part. I'm only getting started."

Jessie crossed her arms and waited for me to continue.

"Her mom offered me fifty grand to walk away."

Jessie's eyes looked like they were going to pop out of her head. "Fifty thousand dollars? First of all, what is this, the 1960s? Secondly, what a bunch of cheapos! A family like that should've offered you five hundred thousand dollars." She slapped my knee. I knew that she was trying to be funny to diffuse the situation, but it wasn't helping.

"I didn't take it. And I wouldn't have taken five hundred thousand dollars either."

"You really love her, don't you," Jessie's voice was quiet, and her eyes searched mine.

"I do." I looked away. "I did."

Jessie rubbed her hand on her jeans. "So what? She was hiding you from her parents. It sounds like she was getting ready to break it to them. Nobody gets photographed in public the way she did if they're trying to hide something from Mommy and Daddy. If you love her, Dylan. You should fight for her."

My teeth were gritted together so hard my jawbone was twitching. "She's pregnant, Jess."

"Oh, my God." Jessie's hand went to her mouth. "I knew it." Her eyes went wide. "I just had this feeling at the game—"

"It's not mine," I interrupted.

Her mouth clamped shut and her eyes went even wider. "What?" her expression of disbelief didn't change.

"Yeah. Does it make sense to you now?"

"Wow." Jessie leaned into the threadbare sofa. "I didn't see that last twist." She tapped her finger on her knee. "It doesn't make sense. Something isn't right."

"I know," I muttered.

"How do you know it's not yours?"

"She told me."

Jess sighed. "I'm sorry, Dylan. This is just so weird."

We both looked at the TV, and while I could see that it was an old episode of *The Simpsons*, all I could think about was the fact that none of this made sense.

"Before you two rekindled your relationship—"

"It was never a relationship before," I clarified.

"Sorry. When was the last time you two were together before this time?"

Itchy and Scratchy were pounding each other with sledgehammers in the background as I thought back to the night in the spring. I had been delivering boats after the ice had gone from the lake. "It was in May."

Jessie nodded. She was thinking the same thing I was. There was a chance this baby could be mine. But there was a chance that it wasn't – and the mother had told me as much.

We sat in silence and watched two more episodes of the cartoon we'd grown up on – laughing at jokes we'd already seen.

"Thanks for coming over, Jess," I stretched my arms over my head. "I needed a quiet night and some laughs."

"Me too." Jessie got up and put on her shoes. "I'm so tired of all this wedding planning. Oh…"

"I guess I don't have a date now." I shrugged. "But I'm not taking your friend," I added quickly.

Jessie laughed. "She's already got a new date and he's perfect for her. They make hummus together."

I followed Jessie to the door and the lights from her ginormous SUV flashed in the kitchen window as she unlocked it from her remote starter.

Jessie leaned on the doorframe. "Kane said that the scouts were writing stuff down after you scored."

"Really?" My heart started to thump against my ribcage. "And you waited two hours to tell me this?"

"You had to get that heartache stuff out of the way to make some room for excitement."

"Are you serious, Jess?" I asked, not wanting to get my hopes up.

"You know I wouldn't make up something like that."

I grabbed my sister and picked her up and squeezed her. "Can you imagine…" I didn't want to finish the sentence.

"I can." She smiled. "And I have. Since you were a kid. Dyl. You're a natural – and lately, you've combined that talent with a little bit of drive – and people are noticing."

I didn't tell Jessie that the reason I started trying harder was to impress Bronwyn. But now, I was doing it for myself and it felt good.

Jessie walked down the concrete steps but turned when she reached the bottom.

"Dyl."

"Yeah." I had my hand on the light switch for the porch, waiting for her to get safely to her car.

"Do you love her?"

I didn't have to think about it. The answer was yes – but that yes had been covered in a layer of anger.

"I always have, and I always will."

Jessie walked back up the stairs and gave me a hug. "If you love her and she loves you – does it matter who the father is?"

I stepped back from the hug and looked at my sister like she'd grown a second head. "Drive safely, Jess."

She pursed her lips, nodded, and then strode to her car.

I couldn't believe that she thought I could entertain the idea of raising another man's child.

It was absurd. Until I thoroughly thought about it.

Floyd was like a father to me. Hell, Andy had been like a father to Jess.

It wasn't an absolute yes, but I went to bed with two very important things on my mind, hockey and Bronwyn.

TWENTY-SIX

BRONWYN

EVEN AT BREAKFAST TIME, the formal dining room was set with linen tablecloths. I was met with the smell of crepes wafting in the breeze when I reached the main house. All the staff was at the estate and Manny, the old butler, opened the door for me.

"Your grandmother is in the sitting room on the veranda, Miss." Manny spoke in a deep, kind voice and bowed his head as I entered.

"Thank you, Manny." I smiled and steeled myself for the first meeting I'd had with the matriarch in months.

I walked through the great room to the formal veranda where my mom and dad were sitting with my grandmother.

"Bronwyn." My grandmother, Eloise stood and motioned for me to come to her. She was a strong, but thin woman, and she squeezed me tightly. Her lavender perfume transported me back to a time when I was young. She'd been wearing the same fragrance her entire life. "It's so nice to see you, sweetheart."

"Nice to see you too, Grandmother."

She smiled and held onto my arms. "You look good."

"Thank you." I was surprised. My mother told me that Grandmother, her mother-in-law wanted to disown me. The warmth Eloise was exuding didn't scream disowning. "You do too."

She grinned. "I still haven't gone under the knife." She cut her eyes at my mother and the dig wasn't lost on me.

"Shall we have breakfast?" My mom walked past the two of us and into the formal dining room.

Grandma Eloise winked at me. "I like to push her buttons."

I smiled and tried to hold in a laugh. "Don't you be doing any of that stuff to your beautiful face." She grabbed my chin and turned my head from side to side. "You're perfect, just perfect."

"Mother." Dad finished his coffee. "That's enough."

Grandmother Eloise waved him off and her silk culottes billowed in the breeze as she walked away. My dad leaned in toward me and whispered, "I think that she's starting to lose it."

If this is what losing it looked like, I was on board. My grandmother was typically all business and very reserved. This warmth was new and it was a little unnerving but also nice. It was as though she'd read a book about what grandparents are supposed to be like and was applying her knowledge to her only grandchild.

Before I could follow my grandmother into the dining room, my dad grabbed my arm. "I need to talk to you." His voice was low and serious.

"About what?" I whispered and glanced around to see what staff might be nearby.

"I met your little boyfriend."

"What?" My heart started to race. "What are you talking about?"

"It doesn't matter. You just need to know that he won't be bothering you again. You need to stay away from that boy."

"I don't think that's going to be a problem." The flash of anger in Dylan's eyes was an image that I wasn't going to soon forget.

"Good." Dad dabbed his mouth with a napkin. "Glad that's all cleared up." He held open the door from the veranda for me. Before I walked through it, a terrible realization dawned on me.

"Did you tell him I was pregnant?"

"No." I believed him. My Dad wouldn't lie to me.

"Oh. Okay."

"Your mother did."

That bitch. "Why the hell did she do that?" I already knew the answer. She was a master manipulator. Of course, she left out the part where Dylan was the father. She knew how to put enough doubt into someone's mind by leaving out key parts to a story.

"She's just looking out for you, Bron."

I crossed my arms across my chest. "We agreed we weren't going to tell him. *You* told me I couldn't tell him."

"Lower your voice," my dad hissed.

My face felt like it was on fire and my hands were shaking. "I have to tell him the truth. Something I should have done from the beginning." I tried to walk into the cottage, but my dad shut the door.

"You should know that your mother offered him fifty thousand dollars to walk away. And he took it."

I felt like the floor was starting to tilt.

"Bron." I could hear my dad's voice. "Help. Someone. Help," He shouted as I dropped to one knee. The world around me blurred and I felt the hands of someone catch me under my arms before the world faded to black.

TWENTY-SEVEN

DYLAN

THE SOUND of an alarm clock always made me feel a rage, so I had been waking up to the local radio station for the past few years. As I blinked my eyes open, the announcer was giving a play-by-play of the events of last night's game.

I wanted to go back to sleep, back to the dream I had been having, but the commentary was too good.

"And Moss scored the goal of the decade. Did you see that fake shot before the tip-in?" the announcer asked his cohost, who wholeheartedly agreed that the goal was magical. Then they took a break from yammering to play some music.

My arms and legs were tired from playing such an aggressive game and I stumbled to shower to let the hot water beat over my tight shoulders. In my dream, Bronwyn and I had been swimming in the lake. She had pulled me to her, and I could feel her feet bumping against mine as we trod water while making out. I had pulled her bikini string and her pink nipples, hard and puckered were bumping against my chest, luminous in the moonlight.

Just the memory of the dream was getting me hard. Even though we weren't together, even though she had hurt me, I couldn't stop myself from thinking about fucking her. I stroked my cock while I imagined slipping inside her warmth while we were in the lake. It was pretty much an impossible feat in real life, but in my dream and in the shower, my cock didn't know the difference.

As I cleaned up in the shower and let the hot water pelt off my face, I heard my cell phone ringing. It was early – and an early call usually wasn't a good thing. I stepped out of the shower and wrapped a towel around my waist.

It was Coach and I was so glad I accepted the call. It was the best early morning phone call I had ever received. The scouts. They wanted to set up a meeting with me.

I got off the phone and braced myself against the bathroom vanity. It wasn't a sure thing, but Coach was optimistic that I'd get invited to the training camp. I held up my hands, they were trembling. I picked up my phone and then set it down – the person I wanted to call with the news wasn't Leo, or Jessie, or Floyd.

It was Bronwyn.

A good night's sleep usually offered me clarity. When I went to bed confused about something, it was like I sorted it out in my sleep. And when I left the house for work, my stomach was clenched into knots. Not the bad kind. I was so excited I couldn't eat.

I was going to play in the National League – and I was going to get Bronwyn and take her with me.

TWENTY-EIGHT
BRONWYN

A LOUD BOAT droned by as I woke up. I was in my bed and by the angle of the sun shining in the window, it was late.

Lisa was sitting on the round chair in the corner. "Miss Bronwyn." She rushed to the bed. "Are you feeling okay?"

"How did I get here?" I smoothed my hands on the sheets. "The last thing I remember…" I racked my brain. It was the conversation with my father. "I can be bought for fifty thousand dollars."

Lisa pressed the back of her hand to my forehead. "You fainted."

"I'm fine." I pulled the sheets back and got out of bed. "What time is it?" I asked.

"It's almost five."

"P.M.? I slept all day?"

Lisa nodded. "The doctor was called in. He said that you just needed some rest, so we let you rest – but if you've got a fever, we have to call him back."

"I don't have a fever." I was pretty sure the redness in my face was due to the memory of the terrible conversation with my father. My mother had betrayed me, and the man I loved, well, he really was after money after all.

Lisa opened the doors to the walk-in closet. "Your grandmother is having the Hutchinsons over for dinner. She's asked that you come for cocktail hour at the boathouse."

I had just fainted and spent the day in bed – now they expected me to put on a pretty dress and smile for some of their business partners. I realized that this was going to be my job. Being a Yates, smiling, and networking. If I was going to continue with the family business, I would have to start acting like them. "How about the pink floral – the wrap-around?"

"Your mom requested something billowy." Lisa mused as she flipped through the hangers in the dress section of my closet.

"Of course, she did." I shook my head and reached over Lisa to pull out a form-fitting red dress.

"Are you sure?" Lisa eyed the dress.

My mom was going to hate it. "I'm sure. Plug in my flatiron please," I shouted as I pulled the dress over my head.

WAITERS WITH BOWTIES offered canapes and glasses of sparkling wine for the small gathering. My lipstick matched my dress and I felt like a model again as I strutted down the pathway to the cocktail hour gathering. After making small talk with the Hutchinsons – a lovely older couple with nineteen grandchildren, we made our way to the dining room. My grandmother still used place cards for sittings, and the table was set as though we were having royalty for dinner, full European settings with the finest china at the estate.

A classical guitarist strummed quietly in the corner as the

first course was served. The Hutchinsons were also in petroleum but were old school enough to never talk about business at the dinner table. It was all talk about the club, the condition of the course, and their boats.

I wasn't paying much attention until the boat being built at the Lake Casper Marina boat was brought up.

"I almost bought it," my dad said.

"It's a beauty," Mr. Hutchinson said. "If you don't buy it, I might. Although, it's a new builder. I'm not too sure about his reputation."

If my mom could've raised her eyebrows at my dad, she would have. "I've heard he doesn't have the greatest reputation." She sipped her wine and glared at me.

"Actually, as a boat builder, I think he's quite talented," my dad replied.

I would've stood up for Dylan, but the fact that he took the money had left me reeling. I picked at the Mesclun salad and hoped that the main course would be a bit more appetizing.

"That's not what I heard." My mom glared at my father. "I've heard that he cuts corners, and the quality isn't that great. He's just some local trying to take advantage of us." This time she looked at me. I gripped the fork tightly, but while she was wrong about the quality, he certainly had taken advantage of the situation with me.

The main course was presented by the bowtie-wearing waiters. The traditional silver domes were removed, revealing that dinner was Lake Casper trout. With the head still on. I pursed my lips and tried not to throw up as the beady little eye stared up at me. I usually enjoyed the fish from the lake, but right now, almost everything made me feel nauseous. I concentrated on the painting of the Woody on the wall as the waiters deboned the fish in front of us.

As the staff filed out of the room, a clatter and commotion came from the kitchen.

"Manny, what was that?" Grandmother sent her butler to find out what was happening.

"My apologies, I don't know what's going on in there," Grandmother's face was flushed. The Hutchinsons didn't seem to care.

"Sir. Sir. You can't go in there." Manny's voice sounded panicked and then the wood-paneled door to the dining room flew open. "Sir," Manny yelled.

It was Dylan.

My dad stood. "What do you think you're doing?"

My mom set down her glass of Chianti so hard it sloshed over the top, leaving crimson drops on the white tablecloth. "Get him out of here," she screeched.

"Wait." Dylan held up his hands and planted his feet wide like a football player about to receive a hit. "I just want to say one thing."

Dad strode to Dylan and grabbed him by the back of his shoulder, like a bouncer. "You need to leave."

"Please, Sir. I just want to say one thing to Bronwyn."

The Hutchinsons' eyes were wide as they took in the debacle. So were my grandmother's. "Peter." My grandmother stood and placed her napkin on the table beside her plate. "Who is this young man? What is going on?

"He's no one," my mom said. "He's just a Laketownie."

My father tried to push Dylan out of the room, but he held his ground. He kept his hands held high and didn't touch anyone, but his voice had grown loud. "Please."

"Peter. Sit down." My grandmother raised her voice – something I didn't think I'd ever heard in my life. My dad let go of Dylan and returned to his chair but did not sit.

"You." She pointed her hand, heavy with diamonds, at

Dylan. "Who are you and why are you interrupting my dinner party?"

"Ma'am." Dylan took off his Otters' hat and looked at me before focusing on my grandmother. "My name is Dylan Moss and I'm in love with your granddaughter."

There's silence and then there's silence. You could've heard a cotton ball fall on a pile of other cotton balls in the dining room.

"You're in love with my granddaughter?" Grandmother looked over her glasses with an amused look on her face. "Bronwyn. Do you know this man?"

"I do." I could've won at poker with the lack of expression on my face.

"Could I have a few words with Bronwyn? Alone?" Dylan's voice was confident, but he was gripping the brim of his hat like an old lady wringing her hands.

My grandmother let out a laugh. "Young man. You don't burst in and interrupt a dinner party like this."

"I'm sorry about that. I just need to talk to her – in person."

"She's part of this family. What you need to say to her, you can say in front of her family."

That was more like the ruthless grandmother of my youth. Although, I was surprised that she wasn't worried about causing a scene in front of her guests.

Dylan cleared his throat and approached me, taking my hand that was resting on the table. I could feel his hand trembling as it held mine, or it was mine that was shaking? At this point, I couldn't tell.

"Bronwyn, I love you. I'm in love with you – all of you."

I could feel every eye in the room trained on us, but I wasn't going to let him come after me for more money.

When I didn't say anything, he licked his lips and continued. "I don't care if I'm the father of that baby or not. I will raise him or her like my own."

My mother stood. "Get him out of here." Her voice was hysterical, and she pointed to the door. "Manny, call the police."

Manny looked to my grandmother for instruction. "Manny, don't do anything – just yet."

"I've heard enough." My mother stood up. "You little piece of trash, you need to get out of here."

"Joan." My grandmother seemed shocked. "What's gotten into you?"

The scene was getting out of control. I pulled my hand from Dylan's and stood. "Grandmother. This is Dylan Moss. He's the father of my child." I watched Dylan as I spoke. His eyes grew wide and filled with tears. "But he's decided to walk away."

"What?" Dylan reached for my hand, but I held it high in the air. "My mother offered this man fifty thousand dollars to walk away from me." The air seemed to get sucked from the room as everyone gasped. "And he took it." I narrowed my eyes at Dylan. "I was only worth fifty thousand dollars to this guy."

"Is this true?" Eloise had taken a seat and had her hands folded on the table in front of her.

"Yes. It's true." Dylan said.

My heart sank.

"She offered me the money, but I didn't take it. She also didn't tell me that the baby was mine. That's news to me."

"You didn't take the money?" My bottom lip quivered.

"Of course, I didn't take the money. I was upset and I was an ass. But Bronwyn, I love you."

It was all I needed. I let Dylan pull me from my seat at the table and in front of my parents, the Hutchinsons and Grandma Eloise, I kissed a Laketownie in the main cottage at the Yates Estate. "Come with me," Dylan whispered in my ear. I glanced around the room, at my tipsy, evil mother, my absentee father, and my confused grandmother, and didn't have to think twice.

"Let's get the hell out of here."

TWENTY-NINE

DYLAN

No one stood in our way as Bronwyn and I fled the main cottage.

"Bronwyn." Now that I could now identify Mrs. Yates' voice, I could tell it was her screeching after us. Her cries echoing down the hallway behind us. "Stop them." Her screams were louder and more panicky sounding. But the staff stepped aside; eyes wide as we hurried through the hall-ways. One of the butlers even opened the main door for us as we reached it.

I held Bronwyn's hand as she trotted behind me in her red heels. She looked curvy and gorgeous in her dress, like an apple, and all I wanted was a bite. A glance told me that no one had followed us to the driveway and my heart was pounding as I pressed Bronwyn against the side of the Volvo and kissed her hard. She moaned into my mouth and pressed her hips against mine.

"I love you, Bronwyn."

"I love you, Dylan," she replied without taking her lips from mine. She kissed me again. "Now, get me out of here."

The two of us sped away from the Yates Estate in a cloud

of dust and smoke. Beside me, Bronwyn let out a combination of a laugh and a scream. "I'm free," she shouted, tears flowing down her face.

The green of the maple and pine trees blurred past the window as we sped towards the highway.

"I can't believe you did that." Her full breasts were heaving with her heavy breaths. "I can't believe you fucking did that!" She arched her head back and screamed again.

I glanced at her to ensure that it was a scream of joy, and the wide cherry red lips in a huge smile confirmed it – joy.

"I would do anything for you, Bronwyn. I was an asshole. I meant what I said back there, but for real – the baby is mine?"

She rubbed her slightly rounded belly. "You're the only man I've been with in years Dylan. This little guy – he's one hundred percent yours."

"I'm going to be a father." My voice shook. "I'm going to be a father," I repeated and turned to look at my beautiful girlfriend. "I'll never let you down – either of you." I slipped my hand from her thigh to her belly, and I could've been imagining it, but I felt a different kind of warmth under my hand. The swelling of my heart was followed by the swelling of desire between my legs.

I glanced in the rear-view mirror and confirmed that there weren't any luxury vehicles in hot pursuit behind us.

"Dylan." She rested her hand on top of mine. "You know that if I'm with you, I'm no longer a Yates. I'm out of the will, disowned…"

The pieces were clicking together, and I nodded. "That's why you asked about the money."

"It is," she whispered. "I was planning to leave everything to be with you."

"You were?" My eyes welled with tears. "You were going to give all of that up for me?"

"I was. I am." The realization of the enormity of what I'd just done was settling in. "The reason I hesitated, Dylan..." her voice was quiet. "I didn't want to put all of this..." she pressed her hand on mine, which was still on her stomach, "on you."

I could see where she was coming from but couldn't believe it. "Bron. I told you, I'd do anything for you."

"I thought that I was setting you free."

"Bron." The tears started to fall. It had been years since I'd actually cried tears – and I don't think that I'd ever cried tears of joy. "This is as free as I've ever felt in my life."

"Me too." She wiped the tears from my cheeks with her thumb and then licked it. "So, we're doing this? You and me?"

As I turned onto my street, the car shuddered, stalled, and then steam hissed out from under the hood. I reached across Bronwyn opened the door and then held her chin as I kissed her. "We are doing this – but you have to make me a promise."

"Anything." She smiled.

"No more secrets." I kissed her softly.

"No more secrets," she murmured.

I got out of the car and pulled her from the passenger seat. "I have one more secret though, one that I can't wait to tell you." I slipped my fingers through hers and pulled her away from the car.

"What's that?" Her heels clicked on the sidewalk as she fell into stride beside me.

"Giving up your fortune for a Laketownie, I can't believe that you did that--"

"We'll figure out a way to get by," she interrupted. "In reality, I have an idea for a business." There was excitement in her voice. "Plus, I learned how to do the laundry and I can make smoothies. I'm sure that I can learn how to cook."

"Whoa, whoa, whoa. I wasn't finished. I would've made it

work, Bron. I would've worked nine jobs for you and our baby."

"I know." Her hair was blowing in the breeze, and she looked like royalty – but in a tight red dress. "But your Lake-townie just got called up to the National League."

She stopped abruptly. "What?"

I turned to face her and held both her hands. "I've been called to training camp. You might have given up billions to be with a poor man, but babe. We're going to be more than okay."

"You know that doesn't matter to me. But Dylan..." She slipped her hands around my waist. "...I'm so proud of you."

I brushed her hair behind her ear. The setting sun had cast an orange glow on her eyelashes. "You've never looked more beautiful." There, on the tiny Laketown side street, I knew that I was going to be with Bronwyn forever. I kissed her and she wrapped her arms around my waist. "I love you more than anything in this world."

"I love you too, Dylan. No matter where we are or what you do. I'll always love you."

The steam from the car stopped hissing by the time we stopped and pulled apart from each other. Cars had been honking at us, but the small Laketown side street and its traffic had disappeared, and it was only us. The three of us.

I tossed the keys to the Volvo on the passenger seat and draped my arm over Bronwyn's bare shoulders.

"Where are we going?" She looked back at the car.

We were a few blocks away. I bent down and took the shoes from her feet and swept her up in my arms.

"Home. Bronwyn. We're going home."

EPILOGUE

TWINKLE LIGHTS SPARKLED HIGH in the rafters of the barn. My heart was pounding against my ribs and the expensive suit I was wearing felt too tight.

"Are you ready for this?" Jessie straightened the bowtie.

"I think I'm supposed to be the one asking you that question," I laughed and wiped the sweat from my brow. It was October, the leaves had changed and at dusk, the temperature was cool – but it felt like a million degrees.

Jessie looked like a Gaelic Princess. Her brown hair tumbled down her back and the diamond tiara shaped like a flower sparkled in the reflection of the lights. "You look perfect." I gave her a hug.

"I wish Mom and Dad were here for this." Jessie's eyes glistened.

The wedding planner counted down, and the first bridesmaid started down the aisle, into the barn.

I took the silk handkerchief from my pocket, a gift from Bronwyn, and handed it to Jessie. "Bronwyn thought these might come in handy. The small white square had a monogrammed M in the corner. "And Jess…"

Bridesmaids two and three were off.

"Mom and Dad. They're here."

Jessie handed the handkerchief to me. "Looks like you might need this too." She dabbed at the corner of my eyes as the first notes of Pachelbel Canon sounded from the harp.

The wedding planner spoke into her headset and then nodded to us.

"Ready?" I whispered.

"Ready." She took my arm and the two of us held our heads high and our shoulders back as we supported each other down the aisle. I kissed my sister on the cheek as I passed her hand to Kane's and took my seat beside my beautiful date – Bronwyn.

As we watched the ceremony, I handed the handkerchief to her, and she held it bunched in her hand on top of her now swollen belly and we threaded our fingers together as we watched Kane and Jessie declare their love for each other.

As the dinner was being cleared, Leo and Brodie Bishop, two of my old Otters teammates joined us at our table. "Congrats, dude." Brodie clapped me on the back.

"Thanks, man. What for?" I grinned. There were so many things in my life that deserved a congratulation.

"Dude. Two years ago, I thought we were going to find you dead in a ditch." Brodie's voice was grim. "Sorry if that's harsh."

"It's okay. It's the truth." I looked at Bronwyn, she knew my history and she reached to hold my hand.

"And look at you now." Brodie poured both Bronwyn and me a glass of sparkling water – I had become a water expert over the past couple of months and preferred an expensive European sparkling water from a specific spring. He held up his glass of champagne and Leo followed suit. "You've been drafted to the New York Thunder, have a gorgeous girl-friend, and are going to be the best dad out there."

Bronwyn slipped the handkerchief into my hand, but I didn't need it. We clinked our glasses together. "To new beginnings."

The group echoed my sentiment and hearing Bronwyn's sweet voice made my heart soar.

Over the past two months, we had grown together as a couple. The first time we made love – the night that I extracted her from the Yates' compound, had been every-thing that I'd imagined and more. Of course, I was nervous about the baby. I was an idiot and didn't know anything, but when I pushed my cock into Bronwyn that night, it was like it was the first time again for both of us. I explored her body with my lips, kissing every square inch of her gorgeous body. I had taken my time with her, thrusting slowly, staring into her eyes, but when I slipped into her from behind, the months and months of waiting, brought out the animal in me. I kissed the back of her neck and she moaned and reached to grab my ass as I thrust into her hard. "Is this okay," I remember whispering in her ear.

"No," she replied.

I almost pulled out, but she gripped my ass and pulled me back in. "Harder."

Our sex life was incredible. No one tells you that making love to your soulmate is going to feel so different. It was as though every night it was new. Almost like our first time – but at the same time, it was like we'd known each other for fifty years. It was fucking perfect.

We left the wedding just after midnight. I wrapped my suit jacket around Bronwyn's shoulders and started the car, a brand-new Yukon, before we left so that it would be warm inside for her.

"Dyl." Bronwyn yawned and stretched her arms over her head. "I'm tired, but there's something I want to show you."

I could've said the same thing to her.

"What is it?" The full moon shone brightly into the cabin of the SUV and cast a glow on top of Bronwyn's existing glow.

"It's at the building site."

"You want to go to the site, tonight?"

"I do," she nodded.

"Whatever you want, Bron." I pulled a U-turn in the middle of the road and headed to Cherry Point Road. The driveway was bumpy and full of ruts from the construction crew and the lights from the car shone on the construction paper covering the workshop.

The advance from the league had been enough to purchase the piece of land on Cherry Point. We were building our dream home – a log cabin on Lake Casper – with space for Bronwyn's new business. The Lake Casper Skin Care line – with its flagship product – Thelma's body butter. Bronwyn had finally convinced Thelma to give her the recipe, and the two of them decided to go into business together.

Bronwyn pulled me by my hand to the shore. "Close your eyes."

I put my hand over my eyes and let her lead me onto the worn planks of the rickety dock.

"Now, open them."

On the shore, topped with a bottle of champagne, sat my boat on a trailer.

"What? How?"

"The buyer," she grinned. "It was me."

"But…" The buyer had purchased the boat for two hundred thousand dollars. "How?"

Bronwyn slipped her hands into mine. "Grandmother

had a change of heart. Turns out she's a sucker for true love. The boat, it's actually from her – a peace offering."

I couldn't believe it. I ran my fingers along the shiny wood and when I rounded the back, I laughed. "You named her?"

"Do you like it?"

She joined me at the stern of the boat. "I love it. The Queen Bee."

Bronwyn handed me the bottle of Cristal. "It's time to christen her."

Together, we held onto the neck of the champagne bottle, her hand on mine, and instead of drinking the ridiculously expensive bottle of wine, we smashed it against the hull of the boat. Bronwyn shivered as I kissed her.

"I know you want to put her in the water, but I'm freezing." It was cold enough to see her breath.

"The boat can wait. There's something better I want to do instead."

She furrowed her brow at me. "What—" but then gasped as I dropped to one knee. I took the ring out of my pocket – a very modest ring from the nineteen eighties – my mother's – and held it up. It was tiny, but it sparkled in the moonlight. "Bronwyn Yates. Will you marry me?"

Her hands clapped to her mouth and her eyes glistened as she nodded. Once she took her hands away, tears spilled from her eyes. "Yes, Dylan Moss. Yes. I will marry you."

I slipped my mother's ring on and kissed her fingers. "It was my mother's."

"It's perfect. I love it. And I love you." I pulled her into my arms and in the light of the harvest full moon, kissed my not secret fiancée.

THE DEFENSEMAN'S SECOND CHANCE

I will never forgive her.

Twenty years is a long time.
Yet, she looks exactly the same.
They say you never get over your first love.
And, I'd have to agree with that statement.
But,
I've also never gotten over my first heartbreak.
And, I don't believe that people change.
The best thing for me - and my heart, is to stay far, far, away
from the new girl in town.

ANDY

I FELT like I was going to puke. But focusing on the puck helped me forget about where I had to go after practice. So, the longer I stayed on the ice, the better. Was I escaping? Sure, that's how I'd used hockey all these years. Once my blades cut through the fresh sheet of ice, whatever was bothering me, anything that existed outside the scuff-marked boards, disappeared.

When the buzzer sounded, I glanced at the scoreboard and wasn't surprised. We had won by three goals. We were still the best team in the league - even if it was just a beer league. But once you're a competitive player, you're always a player.

For an 'old-timer' team we were fast. And with the experience of guys like Dean Covington and other retired Northern Professional League players, I'm pretty confident we could give the local NPHL Laketown Otters a run for their money. Only our muscles bark a little louder than theirs for the next day or five.

O'Malley flicked the puck onto his stick and bounced it a

couple of times before tossing it to the referee. I followed him to the door.

"Oof," he groaned as he leaned to lift the metal bar.

"Back again?" He had taken off his glove and had his hand pressed to his lower back.

"Sciatica."

"You're thirty years old." I stepped in front of my left winger to open the door for him.

Jason O'Malley shrugged. "One too many body checks in the Northern League I guess."

Those who say women have it tough when it comes to aging, must have never met a hockey player. If Jason was old at thirty, I was over the hill at forty.

I turned a blind eye as the box of beer was passed around the room. Technically, alcohol wasn't permitted in the dressing rooms at McManus Place, but I wasn't going to be the guy to take the beer out of beer league.

With the steam of the dressing room behind me, my wet hair froze as I jogged to the mechanical room outside to get to work.

The Zamboni fired up with a strange rattle. I shut off the engine and tried again, breathing a sigh of relief that the sound was gone. As I completed the first pass of the ice resurfacing process, I noticed someone in the stands. I switched the controls from scraping to flooding. When I passed by again my stomach clenched when I realized who had been watching.

The owner of the stadium and my boss – retired hockey legend Jake McManus – sat there. I gave him a casual wave and breathed out a sigh of relief as he smiled and returned it. Maybe he hadn't seen me playing hockey while I was supposed to be working.

After taking a little extra time to make the ice perfect, I

parked and pushed the hydraulic lever to open the giant hood.

"Running a little rough?"

I jumped. "Jake." I cleared my throat. "I didn't hear you come in."

Jake never came into the engine room. I smiled at him and pointed to the engine. I'm going to start with replacing these wires. They operate the…"

Jake held up his hand. "You know I'm not mechanically inclined, Andy. I trust you to take care of it."

"I'll get it sorted out. I was going to do it tomorrow, but I'd be happy to work on it tonight." Please, require me to stay late and fix this damn thing. The thought ran through my mind, and I wished I could say it out loud. I wiped my hands on a towel as I watched Jake survey the ice re-surfacer.

"I don't think that's necessary. I wouldn't want to ask you to miss the funeral."

That's when I noticed that Jake was wearing a black suit under his Otters' team jacket. "I didn't realize that you knew Warner."

Jake let out a sad laugh that almost sounded like a huff. "He was one of the Otters' biggest supporters. He's had a seat in the stands… but I think you know that."

Warner Patterson had been one of my biggest supporters too. He had pushed me to play better. He had believed in me - even when I didn't. He was the main reason I had been drafted to the National League. I couldn't believe that I was looking for an excuse to miss the celebration of his life - he had been a wonderful man. More of a father to me than my own.

"He did love this damn team." I slapped the Otters logo on the side of the Zamboni, trying to distract Jake from hearing the shake in my voice.

Jake nodded. "He sure did."

Then Jake did something I wasn't expecting. He stepped toward me and put his hand on my shoulder. "You can leave early today, Andy. I know that you were close with Patterson." He finished with a squeeze of my shoulder.

"Thanks, man." I gave a little shrug and Jake removed his hand from the shoulder of my work shirt. "We used to be close, but I haven't seen him in years... hadn't seen him." I corrected to the past tense.

"Fair enough." Jake's voice was quiet. "But the offer still stands." He clapped his hands together and started to walk away. "Andy." He paused with his back to me.

I inhaled deeply. "Yeah?"

He turned to face me and the look on his face was serious. The business tone was back in his voice. "There's one more thing."

"Yes, boss."

"What you did on the ice out there..." He pointed to the arena behind me.

I held up my hands and interrupted before he could give me shit. "I know. I shouldn't be playing on work time, but I always stay later on the nights that I do."

A smile broke out on Jake's face. "I don't care, man. That play out there, the one where you faked the pass and dangled the puck..."

I nodded. "It's an oldie but a goodie."

"It was a work of art."

This was not what I was expecting. "Thanks..." I could feel the redness creep out from under my collar. It was a play I could do in my sleep, one that I had perfected during my years as an Otter.

"Andy." He crossed his arms across his chest and his voice seemed to drop an octave.

Was the reprimand coming now? A compliment and then a punishment?

I nodded and shoved my hands in my pockets, my right hand finding my lucky quartz, worn smooth from my thumb over the years.

"I don't care if you play during work hours. I might require it. It would be a shame for skill like that to get rusty."

I studied Jake's face for any hint that he was bullshitting me, but I only saw his trademark grin - the one that had graced the cover of *Sports Illustrated* and many teenage girls' walls during the height of his career. "I mean, if it's part of the job description, I suppose I'd have to do it." I tried to keep the smile from spreading across my face. And for a moment, I forgot about the funeral and the awkwardness that was ahead of me and was grateful that I worked for Jake McManus.

"Right on." Jake pushed the door open but paused as the light from the bright winter afternoon turned him into a dark silhouette. "And Andy, I might join you guys one of these days too. If that's alright."

Jake McManus skating with the old-timers? The idea of it seemed ludicrous – and exciting. "I'll have to check with the guys to see if they want to invite you to tryouts."

His brow screwed up as if he had just eaten something bitter when he was expecting sweet, and his mouth narrowed, but he nodded. "Alright then. Let me know."

"I'm joking." I couldn't hold the laugh in. "Anytime, Jake. The guys will be nervous, so it's best if you just show up – don't give them time to worry about having you on their line."

Jake laughed. "Phew. I used to fall apart in tryouts. Don't sell yourself short, Andy. There are a few guys out there that could jump right onto the line with the Otters. You included." He pushed the door fully open. "See you at the church."

The exhilaration of possibly playing with Jake McManus disappeared when he walked out the door. The church. The

Funeral. Saying goodbye to Warner. The lump in my throat that showed up the day I found out about his heart attack, returned.

There were two reasons I was dreading today The first, and most obvious one, saying goodbye to someone who meant the world to me. The second, the one I didn't talk to anyone about, was that the only woman I ever loved, the only woman who I'd let into my heart and had smashed it like a slap shot to the glass, was going to be there. Warner's daughter, Ellie.

ELLIE

A THICK BLANKET of snow hung precariously from the roof of the bed and breakfast, blocking the view from my window like a heavy blackout curtain. I had been tossing and turning for what felt like hours and when the snow fell to the ground with a loud whoomp. I bolted upright and shielded my eyes with my hand as the sun blasted me in the face.

After two days of meetings with funeral directors and a lengthy visitation the night before, I was exhausted – but still couldn't sleep. I slipped out of bed and pulled the floral curtains together and then crawled back into the sanctity of my duvet cocoon.

My mom died when I was little. I have hazy memories of her, most of them were formed from the photos my dad kept around the house. Growing up without her was hard, but this was harder. It felt like someone had taken a sledge-hammer to my whole world. Thoughts wouldn't stop looping through my brain. Thoughts like if Oliver and I had a baby, he or she wouldn't have actual memories of their grandparents – only photos.

When I finally gave up trying to get some sleep, I pulled

my phone into the bed with me and checked to see if there were any messages from Oliver.

There were no text messages from my husband. My heart sank and I quickly typed him a message:

Were you able to reschedule your meeting? The service is at four.

I pressed send and dropped my phone into the mess of covers. Oliver would show up. He had to; it was my dad's funeral. I padded to the bathroom and turned on the faucets to the old-fashioned claw foot bathtub. While I waited for it to fill up, I splashed some water on my face and tried to recognize the woman in the mirror.

The crying was done. Or at least I thought it was. I didn't think that my body was capable of making any more tears. My eyes were rimmed in red, and the lack of sleep had left dark circles under my green eyes. The electric toothbrush vibrated in my mouth as I stared into the mirror without seeing myself. My father never let me down. And now, in the span of two days, I had been let down by two different men. The worst was Oliver. But I told him that I had everything under control, that I could come to Laketown and do all the arrangements myself – and he had let me. Was that his fault or mine? I should've told him to come, that I needed him. But shouldn't he have known that I needed him there with me?

The visitation had been the night before. I stood at the front of the funeral home with my Aunt Donna and Uncle Raymond shaking hands with what felt like the entire population of the shitty little town. The faces had begun to melt into each other, the *I'm sorry's*, and praises for my father started sounding like a record skipping.

Every time a large man in a suit entered the funeral home, the organ music seemed to slow as I tried to imagine what Andy's face looked like all these years later. The morose music came back into focus louder than ever when I realized it was just another hockey player who I either didn't remember or had never even met. There was a parade of them. Young players with bright eyes who hadn't quite filled into their tall bodies, and older players, the ones my dad would've known, some filled out in the mid-section, their warm eyes surrounded by creases as they either shook my hand or gave me an awkward hug.

As the last of the mourners filed through and returned into the cold winter night, I wondered if I could've missed him. Even though I knew that couldn't be true. There's no way I would ever forget what Andy Bellingham looked like. Even if he'd gained two hundred pounds and lost all his hair, I'd know those icy blue eyes anywhere.

As I'd driven back to the bed and breakfast, I told myself there had to be a reason why he didn't show up. Maybe no one had told him about the visitation. Maybe he'd moved away.

My breath caught in my throat as I imagined the worst scenario. Maybe the first man I'd fallen in love with, the boy who took my virginity in the little cabin on Lake Casper, the one who'd sent me away with a broken heart, had died.

Just to be sure, I rushed to my handbag and pulled out the visitation ledger book, and flipped it open, running my fingertip down the lines, looking for his handwriting. Looks might change, but handwriting didn't, and I knew Andy's.

But his left-handed scrawl wasn't there.

Andy hadn't come.

I sat on the foot of my bed with the book in my lap and let out a big sigh. "It's a good thing he didn't come," I said to myself. He'd hurt me and we'd sworn never to speak to each other again. But part of me didn't think he'd take it this far. He'd loved my dad.

No. He wouldn't let our nasty breakup stop him from celebrating my dad's life.

At least he better not have.

The sound of water hitting the tile floor snapped me out of my thoughts. I slammed the guest book shut and ran to the bathroom where the tub was overflowing. While I mopped up the water, I felt the sadness at both Oliver and Andy's absence slowly morphing into anger. I squeezed the towel into the sink and tried to squeeze away my negativity with the water. Oliver would show up. He was my husband, he had to. And Andy, he had no excuse, my dad was like a father to him. If he didn't show up at the funeral – that fucker better be dead.

End Excerpt

ALSO BY A.J. WYNTER

Windswan Lake

Mine for the Summer

Summer Ever After (Fall 2023)

Hockey Royal Series

Puck King

Ice Queen

Dirty Prince

Laketown Hockey Series

Not a Player

Hating the Rookie

The Coach Next Door

Wingmen are a Girl's Best Friend

The Captain's Secret Baby

The Defenseman's Second Chance

Falling for the Legend

Chance Rapids Series

Second Chances

One More Chance

Accidental Chances

A Secret Chance

Reckless Chances

Titan Billionaire Brothers

CONNECT WITH A.J

A.J. Wynter specializes in small town and sports romance. She left a corporate career in Toronto to move to the mountains and write love stories. Now, she lives in the interior of B.C. Canada with her two dogs and her very own mountain man.

www.ajwynter.com
aj@ajwynter.com

Printed in Great Britain
by Amazon